FIRES OF OLYMPUS

TRIALS 10, 11 & 12: POSEIDON, ZEUS & HADES

ELIZA RAINE

Editors: Anna Bowles, Kyra Wilson

Cover: The Write Wrapping

POSEIDON

THE IMMORTALITY TRIALS

TRIAL TEN

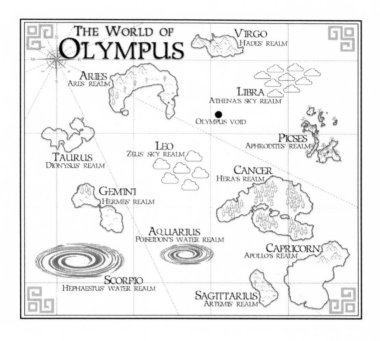

1

ERYX

Eryx's legs were moving before he even realised he was running. He launched himself at the Amazon at the same moment she slashed her sword through the air, only missing Evadne by inches as the blue-haired girl threw herself out of the way. Eryx grunted as he connected with the attacker and she dropped her sword with a clatter as they hit the ground, hard.

'Eryx!' He heard Evadne shout his name over the ringing sound of metal weapons clashing all around them, and he gripped the woman harder and kept rolling, spinning to make sure the writhing, cursing warrior was pinned to his chest. Then an awful wail echoed around them and the woman paused in her struggling. Eryx could see her indecision at the sound of Hippolyta's pain, her hard eyes softening at the sound.

'My Queen!' she gasped, then struggled even harder than before. He tightened his grip, clenching his teeth, forcing out the image of Hercules's bolt thumping into the fierce queen's stomach.

'Enough!' came a bellow from the other side of the courtyard. Such a voice could only belong to a god.

Eryx's muscles went completely slack and his roar of protest and confusion refused to leave his paralysed throat. The warrior woman slid slowly off his chest as an unnatural silence descended.

'Are we all calm now?' a silky smooth female voice asked. 'I think you can let them go, my love.'

Eryx felt control of his body slowly return and he scrabbled to his feet before whirling around to find a weapon before the Amazon could attack again. But before he could find one, she had got to her feet and sprinted away. He checked on Evadne, who was standing at the edge of the courtyard, trembling but safe, then turned back and watched as the Amazon skidded to a halt and dropped to her knees along with a crowd of other warrior women. They were gathered around Theseus and Hippolyta. The queen's clothes were drenched in blood, her face white.

'Aphrodite, my divine love, please help her,' Theseus begged, looking desperately up from Hippolyta's face.

Eryx turned in the direction Theseus was looking and instantly dropped to his knees. Aphrodite and Ares were standing at the back of the courtyard, under a stone arch. The goddess of love looked impossibly beautiful in a floor-length teal gown, her flowing hair an icy pale blue. Ares was in his full warrior gear as usual, his face mostly obscured by his red-plumed helmet.

'That's up to Ares, I'm afraid,' Aphrodite purred. 'What do you think, my darling. Would it be all right if I saved your warrior queen? In the name of love?'

Ares scowled. His hard exposed jaw was scarred and stubbled.

'She was beaten fairly in battle. She should die an honourable death,' he growled.

Aphrodite turned back to Theseus and shrugged.

'There you have it,' she said.

Anguish crossed Theseus's face as he held the bleeding woman. A few of the Amazons stood up, turning to the gods.

'O great Ares, I do not believe the fight was fair,' the woman who had attacked Evadne said loudly. 'This man...' She sneered at Hercules, who was still standing frozen with the belt in his hand. '... attacked with a concealed weapon. And we are to blame. The Amazons fight as a tribe but we were not there to protect our queen. Our shock at her taking a male lover led to her death. We must atone for that.' The woman dropped her head. 'Antiope, her second in command, is already dead. I offer my life too in sacrifice.'

'And mine,' another woman echoed. More and more women stood up, declaring their lives forfeit and Eryx gaped. They loved their queen that much? Would he offer his life for Antaeus's? Once he would have done it in a heartbeat, but now he wasn't so sure. Now, much as he tried to ignore it, there might be another reason for him to live. With an effort, he stopped himself looking at Evadne, keeping his eyes fixed on the gods.

Ares sighed loudly and a slow smile crossed Aphrodite's face.

'Fine! Save her,' Ares snapped. 'I'm not losing my best fighting tribe.'

'With pleasure,' Aphrodite said, her voice silky. She flicked her hand and Hippolyta made an awful gurgling sound, then went completely slack in Theseus arms. His alarmed eyes flicked between the goddesses and the queen. 'She'll wake up healed,' Aphrodite said gently.

'I can't thank you enough,' Theseus whispered.

'Oh, you'll make it up to me,' Aphrodite said, a twinkle in her eye.

'This is supposed to be *my* Trial,' barked Ares angrily. 'And I wanted to let them fight. Why are you doing him favours?'

'I'm sorry, my dear,' the goddess said, turning her beautiful face to him. 'You know how moved I am by true love. Please, take charge.' She gestured at the courtyard, taking a step backwards.

Eryx, along with everyone in Olympus, knew that Aphrodite had many lovers, including Ares and Theseus, and he couldn't help feeling that the god of war had just played right into her hands. Why did she want to save Hippolyta? Or did she just want to please Theseus? He supposed it didn't matter to him, as long as his own crew were safe.

Huge and hulking as they were, Antaeus and Busiris were easy to spot. His captain looked as confused and on guard as Eryx felt. Busiris was beside him, face unreadable, but the brothers, Bergion and Albion, hadn't woken when the calls and shouts of fire had roused the others. They were probably still snoring in their cabana.

'Theseus, you have withdrawn from the competition,' Ares announced. 'Hercules, although your methods are questionable, you are holding the belt. I will award you the win.'

Stony silence greeted Ares announcement.

Hercules bowed his head.

'Thank you, mighty Ares,' he said formally.

'I will transport you back to your ships and you will get the next Trial announcement in six hours, at dawn.'

'Ares, my lord, may I ask one more thing?'

The god's jaw clenched at Hercules's words.

'I do not hand out favours, little mortal,' he growled.

Hercules's neutral expression flickered, but held.

'It is not a favour, so much as a clarification,' he said. 'Hedone left Theseus's crew this morning. To join the *Hybris*. I wanted to be sure you were aware of that.'

Ares took a step forward, his hand moving to the sword hilt at his hip, but Aphrodite quickly laid a hand on his shoulder.

'We are aware of everything, Hercules. Hedone will return with you to the *Hybris*,' she said.

Hercules bowed his head low.

'Thank you, divine ones.'

Eryx turned instinctively to Evadne. It was as Busiris had said. What would happen to her on that ship now? He caught a glimpse of the dread showing on her face, before the world flashed white and he was back on the deck of the *Orion*.

2

LYSSA

Fury rolled through Lyssa as she paced the deck of the *Alastor*. How? How had he won? And so unfairly! How could the gods be so twisted, so cruel, so unjust? These were the same thoughts that had consumed her after Hercules had emerged punishment-free from his trial after killing her family, and she was aware how easily they could consume her again. But the anger was surging inside her, building into something she knew she couldn't contain. *Antiope, Epizon's mother, impaled on* Keravnos, *Hippolyta pale and soaked in blood in Theseus's arms, her mother...* Red began to tinge her vision and her hands felt like they were too big, too powerful for her body. *Hercules, holding the belt and his glowing sword, his lion-skin cloak spattered in the blood of others.* Energy, massive and unyielding, was starting to flood her veins, and her head was beginning to pound.

'Epizon!' she sent the desperate thought to her first mate.

'Captain?' his mental reply came instantly.

'Epizon, I'm going to kill him. I'm going to kill him, and then I'm going to make them all pay.'

'Lyssa, calm down.'

'They can't play with us like this! They can't rule an entire world like this!' She was unable to stop herself shouting the words aloud. 'We're like damn toys to them!'

'Lyssa?' She whirled around at the sound of Phyleus's voice. He was walking slowly across the deck towards her but paused as he saw her expression. Uncertainty flashed across his face.

'They will all pay,' she growled.

'They will. But not tonight,' he said quietly.

She let out a cry of frustration, guttural and feral and filled with the torrent of power that was building inside her but that she could not use.

'You don't understand! You can't know what this feels like.'

'Tell me,' Phyleus said, stepping closer to her. She stared at him, her heart hammering, her skin burning.

'I'm in a body that's too small for me. I have the strength, the power to make bad people pay for what they've done, but I'm useless. I can see the people I love dying around me, can see people I care about losing everything. I can see blood and death and greed winning over all else but I can't stop it, even with all this power.' Tears of frustration made her eyes hot as she spoke, the truth of what she was saying almost physically painful.

'You feel like a tidal wave smashing harmlessly against rocks. Or a tornado trapped in a box. Or a raging fire only an inch tall.' Power continued to surge through Lyssa as Phyleus's words rang through her.

'Yes,' she whispered. 'Exactly.'

'Lyssa, you are going to make a difference to this world. You're going to stop that sick man from becoming immortal and that alone will save countless lives. Your power *will* be released. And you will use it for all the right reasons, against all the right people.'

She drew his words into her, trying to make them louder than the blood rushing to her head as the Rage teetered on the edge of taking over. 'And when this is over, when you've saved the world,' he went on, 'we'll have a lifetime of sailing the skies, together.'

She stared into his warm brown eyes, and for a moment she could almost feel the wind in her hair as she soared through the clouds, her hand clasped in his, the world far beneath them. The red seeping into the edges of her vision leaked away. 'No more pressure. No more feeling alone. No more anger.' He stepped close to her, taking her hand as it started to tremble.

'You really think we can have that?'

'I know we can.'

She stepped up to press against him, her mouth finding his before she could register what she was doing. Her Rage morphed and whirled around inside her, desire, not just for him but for the life he'd just described, filling her completely. He kissed her back, hard, and she was vaguely aware that she needed to control her strength. 'I will do anything to help you, Lyssa,' he said, breaking their embrace and moving far enough back to look into her eyes. 'Anything for a life with you.'

'Why?'

'I love you.'

The short, simple sentence rocked Lyssa, pounding through her overwhelmed brain. Love? How could he love her after only knowing her for a such a short time?

But she knew it was true. She could see it in his eyes, feel it in his kiss, hear it in his words. And more than that, she felt it too. They had a bond that went deeper than the spark of chemistry she'd felt between them when he'd first joined the ship. Something uncontrollable and undeniable. Something real. Emotion and energy ricocheted through her, and she realised her need for revenge and retribution was paling beside her need for him.

'I need you,' she breathed. His mouth quirked in a half-smile.

'Not quite *I love you too* but I'll take it,' he said. 'Save your Rage. We'll beat him in the next Trial. And then we'll celebrate.'

She stared at him.

'I'm starting to think you don't fancy me,' she said.

'Ohhh, I do. I very much do,' he said, taking her hand and brushing it against the front of his trousers. Desire pulsed through her so hard her head hurt as she felt him. He was telling the truth. He *did* want her. 'But I don't want our first time together to be an outlet for your anger.'

He was right. Rage shouldn't be what brought them together like that. But she needed to do something with her power, before she exploded.

'In that case, I'm taking my ship for a spin. You might want to hold onto something,' she said.

HERCULES

'I knew you'd win!' Hedone's husky voice was full of excitement as she threw her arms around Hercules's neck. He wrapped his own around her waist and lifted her up to him, kissing her deeply. Not only had he won, but he'd eliminated his biggest competition. With Theseus out of the Trials, immortality was as good as his. And at last, his beautiful Hedone was on the *Hybris* with him. Excitement spread like fire through his body.

'Of course I won, my love.' He set her back down on her feet and strode across the plush carpet of his living quarters to the bar, where he began to pour them both a drink.

'What are you going to do with the belt?' she asked him as he handed her a glass of ouzo. He scowled at it.

'Keep it as a trophy of my victory,' he said.

'A gift from Ares shouldn't be wasted. What do you think it does?' Hedone was staring at the belt. Did she want it?

'Anything made by the god of war has no place on

your beautiful body,' he told her. She smiled at him. 'You don't need to be anything like those warrior women.'

He lifted Hippolyta's belt from where it lay on the couch and walked over to a large mahogany chest by the bookshelves. Dropping the ugly thing into the chest, he closed the lid. It could be displayed in his home after the Trials. For now he wanted no further reminder of that brutish woman. How Theseus could possibly love such a person was utterly beyond him. What a fool the pretty man was, to give up an eternal life for a chance to save a woman who didn't even want to be with him.

'I'm so happy to be here,' Hedone said, drawing his attention back to her.

'As am I. I'm sorry we couldn't get any of your things from the *Virtus*,' he replied.

She shrugged.

'I don't need them. I just need you.'

'I'll have Evadne bring you her clothes. You can choose what you'd like.'

'She's smaller than me; I doubt much will fit.'

Hercules pictured the slight, blue-haired girl. It was true, she was nowhere near as curvy or voluptuous as Hedone.

'They will have to do for now. We shall buy some clothes, just as soon as we can.'

'We should get some rest. The next Trial will be announced in a few hours,' Hedone said softly.

Hercules knew there was no way he would sleep. But he was more than happy to take Hedone to bed. Her eyes sparkled as they saw his own fill with lust.

'My bed is yours,' he growled, gesturing to his

bedroom. She bit her full bottom lip as she raked her gaze over him, and his body responded instantly. He downed the rest of his drink, relishing the fiery feeling as it burned through his chest, and followed her swaying hips into his bedroom.

Everything was going to plan, at last.

EVADNE

E vadne couldn't bring herself to knock on Hercules's door as she arrived with her arms full of clothes. She didn't want to see him. She didn't want to meet his eyes, in case her feelings showed on her face. He revolted her. He terrified her. She couldn't understand how she hadn't seen him for what he was months ago, and she hated herself for it.

She laid the clothes down outside the wooden door. Most of them wouldn't fit Hedone. Evadne favoured tight-fitting leather fighting gear, and the garments would simply be too small for the curvy woman. But most of the dresses could be altered.

Any resentment she felt towards Hedone for helping herself to her wardrobe was overshadowed by her desire to get off the *Hybris*. Hercules had no need for her any more, and she didn't want to find out where that would lead. She had almost finished folding the clothes neatly in a pile on the floor, intending to sneak off and leave them there, when the door creaked and swung open. It was Hedone, and she jumped at finding someone right outside.

'Oh! Hello,' she said. Evadne blushed. The woman was wearing nothing but Hercules's shirt, and her olive skin was flushed and glowing. She was stunning. 'I was on my way to the galley. Where is it, please?'

Evadne pointed.

'The fourth door on the left,' she mumbled.

'Is that Evadne?' Hercules's voice came from inside the room and Evadne's skin instantly began to crawl.

'Yes,' replied Hedone.

'Good. Send her for the food.'

'Oh. OK.' The beautiful woman turned back to Evadne. 'May we have something to eat?'

'Something hot,' Hercules called.

'Um, sure,' Evadne said, and hurried away down the corridor.

She was heating some leftover slices of beef pie in one of the many ovens in the long galley when Hercules stepped into the room. Her breath caught as his cold grey eyes fell on hers, and her pulse quickened.

'I've been trying to talk to you through mind-speak,' he said quietly. 'But I can't reach you.' Her skin felt too tight and she concentrated on keeping her face a mask. 'Do you know what that means, Evadne?'

She did. It meant she was no longer part of the crew. She had rejected the ship, and it her.

'No, Captain,' she lied.

'It means that I have very little need for you on board the *Hybris* any more. It means I don't trust you,' he hissed, taking a step towards her. She visualised the work surface behind her, trying to remember exactly where she'd put the knife she'd been using on the pie.

'I'm just heating your food,' she said, unable to think of single other thing to say. He stared at her and she felt sick as she tried not to hold her breath.

'You will not be joining me on the next Trial,' he said eventually. Hope blossomed inside her. If he left her on the ship while he took part in the Trial, she could leave, and take what she needed with her.

'As you wish, Captain,' she said.

He moved forward before she could blink, reaching past her and scooping the knife off the countertop. She whirled out of the way, backing against the wall of cupboards, moving sideways towards the door.

'You will stay on the *Hybris* and you will do exactly as you are bid. Do you understand me?' His voice was barely audible as he stepped towards her, his massive chest expanding as he pointed the knife at her throat. She nodded quickly. 'You are now my servant. You will service me and Hedone and you will ask no questions. In fact, you will not make a sound.' Her heart hammered against her ribs as she nodded again. He lunged forward and she darted to her left under his arm. He caught her swinging ponytail, though, and yanked her backwards. 'Clearly, you do *not* understand me!' he exclaimed, a twisted grin contorting his handsome face as he lifted her by her hair to face him. Pain lanced through her skull. 'I just told you that you are here to serve me. Not run away from me!' He dropped her to the ground and she stumbled, falling onto one knee. She felt him grab her ponytail again and struggled quickly to her feet, trying to stop him pulling.

'I'm sorry,' she whispered.

'And I told you not to make a sound. Let me show you what happens when you disobey me, Evadne,' he said, and dragged her in front of the shining metal cabinets lining the end wall. She saw tears spilling from her eyes in her reflection as he sawed the knife through the fistful of her hair he was holding.

'Next time, it will be something that doesn't grow back,' he spat as he leaned close to her ear. 'Hurry up with that pie,' he said, and threw her ponytail onto the floor as he stalked out of the galley. Evadne stared at her reflection a long time after he was gone, her blue hair hanging unevenly to her jaw and her cheeks wet with silent tears.

She had to get off the *Hybris*.

5

LYSSA

Lyssa stared at the orange flames in the fire dish, her eyes heavy and unfocused. She was so, so tired. After waking the entire ship with her Rage-fuelled blast through the skies she had retired to her room, exhausted. The few hours' sleep she'd managed to get were nowhere near enough, but she'd had no choice. She hadn't been able to contain her Rage.

The flames flashed white and she sat up straight, shaking her head to clear it.

'My money's on Poseidon,' muttered Len beside her. 'They'll save the big two until last.'

'Good day, Olympus!' If Lyssa ever met that smiley announcer, she would punch him square in the face. 'Well, things are really livening up now, aren't they? Let me just remind you of the scores. There are only three crews left now and the *Orion* has two wins, the *Alastor* two, and the *Hybris* is in the lead with three. Can Hercules win another? Let's find out...' His beaming face faded away, replaced by that of Poseidon, his piercing aqua eyes intense.

'Told ya,' said Len triumphantly.

'Heroes. Journey to Aquarius. There your ships will be altered to sail underwater.' Lyssa's mouth fell open as the silver-haired god spoke. The *Alastor* underwater? 'The sea-shepherd Geryon has a well-guarded flock of hippocampus. Capture one of his pets and bring it to my throne room. The first to do so will win.'

The second Poseidon vanished, Lyssa felt the ship lurch to life. She looked at Abderos. The excitement showing on his face forced a smile to spring to her own.

'Underwater, Cap! Can you imagine!'

'It'll be a new experience, for sure,' she said.

'Do you think it matters how fast we get there? Do we need a boost?' Epizon asked.

Lyssa shook her head, guilt washing through her. She'd burned all her energy hours ago, in useless anger.

'Sorry, Ep. I have to sleep. The *Alastor*'s fast enough without me, though. We'll keep up.'

'We sure will,' said Abderos. 'We'll be there in about eight hours, I reckon.'

'Good. Only wake me if there's an emergency,' she said, and got up from the captain's chair.

LYSSA SLEPT LIKE THE DEAD, until she was woken by a hammering on her door. She groaned loudly.

'We'll reach Aquarius in half an hour, Captain,' came Epizon's voice. She yelled back an incomprehensible sound and forced her eyes open with a sigh. They needed to win this one. Or at least stop Hercules from winning it. He would be dangerously far in the lead if they didn't.

She washed and dressed quickly, and tried to ignore the disappointment she felt that she hadn't heard Phyleus's voice in her mind since she awoke. *I love you.* He'd really said those words. Did she love him? There was no doubt she wanted him. And she couldn't help the swell of hope and yearning she felt when she pictured the life he described. A life together. She needed to pull apart her feelings, try to work out why the prospect of living her life with Epizon and the crew had never made her feel the way Phyleus did. Try to work out why she was resisting him. But her focus was needed elsewhere now. Maybe that was why he hadn't spoken to her.

'Morning, Cap,' said Abderos as she strode onto the cargo deck.

'Morning, Ab,' she said, nodding at him. She scanned the deck quickly for Phyleus. He was with Epizon, leaning over the railings under the huge sails. He glanced up at her and her stomach flipped.

'Hi,' he said in her head.

'Hello.' *I love you.* The words echoed in her mind.

'Sleep well?'

'Yes. Get up here and bring Epizon,' she said, forcing herself to stop staring at him.

'Aye, aye, Captain.'

SHE ROUNDED up Len and Nestor, and when everybody was gathered on the quarterdeck she spoke.

'This is the most important Trial so far. If Hercules

wins this one, then he's as good as won the whole thing. Theseus was our best ally and a strong competitor, so him being out is only going to make this harder. The whole ship is taking part and I need everyone to obey my commands without question. Understood?' Her eyes fell on each of them in turn as they nodded. She lingered on Phyleus. 'You especially,' she said.

'As if I would disobey orders,' he answered in mock indignation, and Abderos laughed.

'I mean it,' she said seriously.

'Of course, Captain,' he said, his smile falling away.

'We have to stop him winning this one.'

The tenth labour Hercules was given was to capture the cattle of Geryon from an island surrounded by ocean. Geryon was descended from the Titan Oceanus. He had three bodies that all joined as one at the stomach and his cattle were exceptional.

EXCERPT FROM

THE LIBRARY BY APOLLODORUS

Written 300–100 BC

Paraphrased by Eliza Raine

6

HEDONE

Hedone leaned over the railing of the *Hybris*, the wind picking up her skirts as she inhaled the salty scent of the ocean. With a couple of slight alterations, quite a few of Evadne's dresses had fit her. This one was a sage green, lined with cream. It was cut higher across the chest than the ones she usually wore but she liked it well enough.

They were moving lower as they approached Aquarius, sailing just a few feet above the waves. The only indication that they had reached the realm at all was the intense glow that rippled across the churning surface of the water.

She had never heard of Geryon, the shepherd, but she had seen hippocampus before. They had a horse's head, chest and front legs, which merged into a fish's tail, a lot like a mermaids, and a long, shimmering fin that ran all the way down their spine. They were not intelligent or evolved, and back in Pisces many were tamed and could be ridden.

The thought of her home realm made her frown. Where would she and Hercules live when this was over? She didn't want to go back to sharing her friends and social life with Theseus. So she guessed that meant Leo. She wondered what Hercules's home looked like. Would she like it? Would he live somewhere else if she didn't?

A beam of light suddenly shot up from the ocean ahead of them, bright purple. She squinted into the glare, and saw the battered old Crosswind owned by Captain Lyssa fly straight into the beam before shooting downwards, under the water. Then a white light burst up next to the purple one. Hercules's colour in this competition was white, she remembered.

'Hold onto something, my love,' Hercules shouted from his chair on the rear quarterdeck. She didn't think she wanted to be at the railings if they were about to be sucked under the water, so she turned and ran towards him, taking the steps two at a time. He smiled at her as she reached him.

'You're fast,' he said.

'I can move.' She grinned. 'I think I'm safest here with you.'

'I agree.'

She moved to stand behind his chair and gripped his huge shoulders firmly as they sailed into the light.

THE SHIP DIDN'T TILT as it plummeted downwards, instead dropping like a stone. Before she had time to worry about drowning, though, the water crashed against an invisible barrier, like a dome around them. In seconds, they were completely submerged, light shining through the surface of the ocean above them. She gaped as she looked up, watching the light dim as they sank deeper.

'Can you still control the ship?' she asked.

There was a pause before Hercules answered, 'Yes,' and the *Hybris* lurched to the left. Hedone stumbled slightly, and Hercules's arm shot up to grip hers, stabilising her.

'Thank you,' she said, and leaned forward to kiss his cheek.

'Captain.'

Hedone looked up to see the minotaur stepping off the stairs onto the quarterdeck.

'Asterion,' Hercules said. 'Do you know Geryon?'

'I know of him, Captain. He is well respected in my circles.'

'Excellent. Do you know where he is?'

'I do, Captain.'

ONCE THEY HAD BEEN under the water five minutes or so, Hedone felt safe enough to return to the railings. She daren't put her hand up to the invisible dome, but she wanted to watch their entrance into Aquarius. She loved visiting the underwater realm, although she had never approached it like this before.

The usual way of visiting was via special haulers that floated on the surface of the ocean in narrow towers. From here, though, she could see the hundreds of domes resting on huge slabs, hovering a hundred feet under the surface. Each one glowed with its own light, and was filled with white stone buildings. As they approached she could make out the triangle shapes of the ancient-style temples, and the network of horizontal haulers that connected the domes together. She could see a market-place as they soared right over the top of the outer domes, filled with people going about their daily busi-ness. Mer-people and other sea-folk were popping through the dome's edge, not needing the haulers to move around. She felt a pang of jealousy.

She remembered that the marketplaces in Aquarius had some of the most beautiful jewellery in all of Olym-pus. But, gods, how her life had changed since her biggest excitement had been shopping! Changed for the better, though. She glanced at Hercules, regal-looking in his lion skin, on his red-lined chair. *Definitely* changed for the better.

They continued to soar over the domes of Aquarius until they reached the outskirts on the opposite side, where the domes were larger, but less populated. Wildlife from above-ground, like cows and pigs, lived in many of them, and they acted as underwater farms, providing for the families in the main city. The cattle looked odd and out-of-place, tinged with blue. As beautiful as Aquarius was, Hedone didn't think she could live in a world where real, fresh air was so inaccessible.

Eventually, they came to an area where barely any domes were visible. There was a giant net, though, that seemed to start in the dark depths of the ocean, and stretch all the way up to the surface. Hedone couldn't see the edges; it just seemed to go on forever in each direc-tion. The net shimmered and shone, a bit like the solar sails of the ship. She looked up at the *Hybris*'s sails, which were currently sparkling blue, the rippling light of the ocean reflecting and bouncing off them so that it almost seemed like they were made from liquid themselves.

She looked back at the net, and a shining flash beyond it caught her eye. It was a hippocampus, but the creature was different to the ones she was used to. It was as iridescent as the sails and net, covered in plating that looked like mermaid scales shining every colour of the rainbow. Where its hooves should have been were webbed toes and the long fin on its spine rippled as it moved gracefully through the water.

'It's stunning,' she breathed.

'It's our ticket to immortality,' said Hercules, standing up.

7

HERCULES

Hercules felt *Keravnos* hum to life in his hand as he looked out past the massive net.

'Asterion. Hold the ship steady by the net,' he instructed the minotaur.

'Yes, Captain.'

Hercules strode over to Hedone and kissed her.

'I'll be back in a moment. Stay here.'

Then he took off at a run, leaping onto the railings and launching himself through the barrier around his ship. The water was cool but not freezing, and he powered through it towards the net. He drew *Keravnos* as he kicked, and slashed at the net. There was a moment's resistance, then the sword melted through the material like it was nothing.

He slashed a few more times, making the hole as wide as he could, before kicking his way back to the *Hybris*, where he grabbed the railing and pulled himself through the invisible barrier, taking a deep breath as he left the water. It took him three trips to cut a hole in the net big enough for the ship. When he pulled himself onto the deck the third time Hedone was pointing at something behind them, a worried look on her face. Seeing what had caught her attention, he snarled, running his hands through his wet hair. The *Alastor* had followed them.

'Let's go!'

The ship shuddered forward in response to Hercules's bellowed command, angling towards the hole in the glowing net. A loud swishing noise made Hercules spin on the spot. He couldn't work out where the sound had come from, but it was like something being dragged through liquid. He heard it again, from his other side and he whirled around, raising *Keravnos*. Hippocampus were starting to come into focus all around him now. They were so bright and shiny, it was impossible to miss them. Catching them would be like shooting fish in a barrel.

The thought made him pause. What if he did shoot them? They needed to take a live creature to Poseidon's throne room, but if he captured one and then killed the rest... nobody else could win.

'Asterion, man the ballistas. On my mark, shoot the hippocampus.'

'What? Why?' asked Hedone, her big eyes full of concern.

'It is the easiest way to win, my love.'

'But... They're innocent. And so beautiful.'

A pain blossomed in his chest, unlike anything he had felt for a long time. She was so... good. So kind. She didn't understand how cruel the world needed to be. And he didn't want to be the one to tell her. But he had no choice.

'Innocence is a gift, Hedone; one that few of us can indulge in. The hippocampus are ignorant. They will feel no fear or pain and they will be contributing to a much higher cause.'

She stared up at him, then gave a small nod. Suddenly her eyes focused on something behind him and widened in fear. He turned and froze. The creature looming over the *Hybris* was almost as big as the ship. It had a man's chest and three human-looking heads, each with a green spiked crown growing like horns around masses of dark hair. Four arms protruded from its chest, each ending in vicious-looking claws like a crab's, and behind it towered dark green, leathery arched wings. Instead of legs, the thing had a tail like that of a serpent, covered in long sharp barbs and seemingly unending.

'You have broken through my net,' the central head boomed. 'You will not steal my cattle!' The creature swiped with his tail so fast that Hercules barely had time to command the *Hybris* to move out of the way. The momentum of the swipe rocked the ship and they all stumbled and scrabbled as they lurched.

'Hedone, go to my quarters. You will be safer there,' he said as he gripped her wrist and steadied her. She started to protest but he fixed his eyes on hers. 'For me, my love. Please. I can't fight well if I'm concerned for your safety.'

'OK. But be careful,' she said, then turned and ran for the hauler. Hercules turned back to the monster, ready for the fight, and couldn't help the bark of glee that erupted from him. Geryon was whipping his tail at the *Alastor* now. The tiny ship darted out of the way and all three of Geryon's heads roared, before he swooped after them.

'Asterion, man those guns,' Hercules ordered, fixing his eyes on the closest hippocampus.

8

LYSSA

Lyssa laid her hands on the mast, her body tingling as the *Alastor* drew on the Rage swirling through her. She let Abderos direct the ship out of the monster's path, and concentrated on only letting a trickle of power boost the ship; enough that they could outrun Geryon but not so much that they would be overwhelmed. Why hadn't the stupid creature gone for the *Hybris* instead of them? The sense of injustice made her Rage surge up and the ship shot forward. She heard Len yelp and Epizon's voice rang through her mind.

'Easy, Captain!'

'Sorry,' she answered 'But what are we going to do? We need to catch one of those hippocampus.' She projected the last thought to everyone on board.

'There's probably enough stuff in the cargo deck for us to make some sort of net,' suggested Phyleus.

'Really? You think we have time to make a net?'

'Do you have any better ideas?' The *Alastor* rocked as

Geryon flashed past them, his wings almost touching the mast. Lyssa released a burst of power and they darted to the right.

'No, but I don't know how long we can keep this up,' she said.

'Try to draw him over to the *Hybris*. See if he wants to play with them for a little while instead,' Len said.

'Good idea. Ab, head towards the *Hybris*. Everyone else, go and see what you can find in the cargo deck.'

She heard a chorus of 'yes, Captain,' in her head as the massive serpent tail flicked past on her left.

'You're doing great, Ab,' she told him as they veered away.

'Thanks, Cap. You're doing pretty good yourself!'

She squinted ahead of them, but from her low position in the middle of the ship, at the mast, she couldn't see the *Hybris*. This was not the start to the Trial she had hoped for. When they'd spotted the *Hybris* moving with such purpose and guessed its crew knew where Geryon's hippocampus were, they thought they'd lucked out, and followed at a safe distance, letting Hercules do all the hard work for a change. So how in the name of Zeus had they ended up as a toy for this great winged beast while Hercules was free to try to catch a hippocampus?

'Cap, I think we can make something from the crates themselves. Maybe lower them over one or something.'

Lyssa frowned at Len's voice.

'That sounds pretty flimsy. Maybe I should just swim out and grab one.'

'Just grab one?' Phyleus sounded shocked. 'Lyssa, you

can't just grab a hippocampus. Do you know how strong they are?'

'Not as strong as me. And it's *Captain*, not *Lyssa*,' she fired back.

9

ERYX

E ryx took a deep breath, and pushed himself off the railings of the *Orion*. As usual, they were late to the party, but they'd got there in time to see the shape of a ship in the distant blue, and follow it.

When they arrived at the net, both the *Hybris* and the *Alastor* were on the other side. Hercules was swimming after a skittish, shining hippocampus, more beautiful than any that Eryx had ever seen. A massive creature with three heads and tall wings was swishing around the *Alastor*, whipping its barbed tail at the ship as it zipped around. It looked almost like they were dancing, he thought as he launched himself from the side of the ship and kicked through the water towards the hole in the net.

Antaeus powered past him, his legs that much bigger and stronger.

For ten full minutes they tried to widen the hole enough to get their giant Zephyr through it, swimming back and forth between the net and the *Orion* to get more air, but neither of them were making much progress. The glimmering fabric was insanely strong, and try as he might, Eryx could not tear it with his fists.

He thought about Hercules killing the Amazons, throwing the boy from the *Alastor* to the horses, grinning with savage glee when he'd killed the centaurs at the feast before the Trials started. He thought of the fear on Evadne's face when he'd last seen her before they were flashed out of Themiscyra.

Anger and determination sent strength surging through his muscles and he felt the fabric finally give a little. He glanced over at Antaeus, who had managed to widen the hole by about a foot, then back at the huge *Orion*. They would be here forever. Frustration made him screw his face up, bubbles of air escaping his mouth. He kicked his way back to the ship, where he pulled himself back on board and took a few deep breaths.

'We're never going to get through like this,' snapped Busiris.

'We might if you got off your ass and helped,' Eryx spat back, pushing loose strands of his long hair out of his face.

'I don't swim,' Busiris sneered.

'Then it's time you learned.'

'Enough.' Antaeus's voice cut across them as he landed on the deck with a thud. 'Change of plan. We guard this hole, and when that lowlife coward comes through, we steal his hippocampus.'

'What?'

'Look.' Antaeus pointed, and Eryx followed his finger. Hercules was rolling through the water, a struggling hippocampus wrapped in his huge arms. Hercules, although not as big as Eryx, was still big enough to wrestle it effectively. They were just above the *Hybris*, and Eryx watched as Hercules rolled over and over, forcing both himself and the animal towards the ship.

As they reached the invisible dome the hippocampus began to flail wildly, then the two of them were falling fast to the deck. There was a loud bang and one of the many other shining creatures on the far side of the net shot backwards, then began to drift slowly downwards, unmoving.

'What's happening?' Eryx frowned as another hippocampus did the same.

'He's killing the others,' drawled Busiris. 'Smart. Very smart.'

Eryx turned to him in disgust.

'There's no need to kill them!'

'If he has the only live hippocampus it massively increases his chance of winning,' Antaeus said darkly. 'We wait for him here.'

10

LYSSA

'Cap, I think we have a problem.' Abderos's voice cut through Lyssa's concentration as she funnelled more power into the *Alastor*.

'Gods, what now?'

'Hercules is killing the hippocampus. And I can't get close to his ship with those ballistas firing.'

'What? Why would he kill them?'

'I think he's caught one. It's hard to tell, I'm trying to steer and keep an eye on him at the same time.' As he said the words a massive wing clipped the side of the ship and they rolled dangerously far to the right. Lyssa gripped the mast hard.

'Nestor!' She half-bellowed the thought at the centaur.

'Yes, Captain?'

'Get up here now, I need a lookout.' Nestor was up on deck in less than a minute, galloping past her to the prow. 'Ab, sail over the *Hybris*, as close as you can. Nestor, has Hercules caught a hippocampus?' The ship veered upwards and Lyssa loosed a burst of energy to propel them past Geryon's snapping claws.

'Yes, Captain.'

Lyssa bared her teeth.

'Geryon is going to get bored of playing with us when he realises his pets are dying. We need options, now.'

There was a roar from somewhere nearby and then the *Alastor* lurched harder than it had so far. Lyssa's hands were knocked from the mast and she stumbled sideways.

'Captain, there's water down here!' Epizon's voice shouted in her mind, as Geryon swooped over the ship. She looked up at him, all three sets of gleaming blue eyes fixed on her as his tail came hurtling towards them. She threw herself forward, plunging all her Rage into the ship the second her hands made contact. The *Alastor* darted forward so fast she was thrown from the mast again, but its momentum, and Abderos's skill at the wheel, kept the ship moving, heading up.

There was an ominous creaking sound and Lyssa turned her head as Nestor yelled, 'Look out!'

The sound of galloping hooves rang out over the creaking as Lyssa struggled to her feet, then she was bowled over by Nestor's huge white horse body, as the main mast came crashing down onto the deck, right where she'd been standing. Lyssa rolled, physical pain tearing through her as the glittering solar sails collapsed around her, obscuring everything from view. She felt the mast splitting like her own body was breaking, smashing the planks as it fell as if her own bones were being pulverised.

'Lyssa! What's happening?' Phyleus's voice pierced through her pain and she clung to it.

'The *Alastor*!' she said desperately. 'We have to save her!' She was on her knees, trying to work her way out from under the heavy sails, the ship still lurching and shaking. Tears were filling her eyes as she felt the broken planks under her hands, felt the ship's straining energy ebbing away. She roared, forcing her own strength and power into the wood beneath her palms, willing the ship to rise. 'The surface,' she told the *Alastor*, as fiercely as she could. But without the main sails, the ship only shuddered and heaved. 'Please,' she begged, pouring more and more of herself into the ship as the tears spilled from her eyes and onto the wood. 'Please. I need you!'

And then she felt the ship rising, the fallen sails pressing down on her as they rushed upwards through the ocean.

11

EVADNE

Evadne's breath caught as the *Hybris* reached the hole in the net. She had sneaked up to the front quarterdeck, which she knew would be empty, and was crouched between the railings and the front wheel, watching and waiting for the right time to act.

She didn't think this was it. The *Orion* was pressed up against the fabric net, the opening guarded by the three huge full giants and Eryx, his fists clenched, bouncing from foot to foot. She heard Hercules roar and the ballistas start firing.

'You're not strong enough to fight me, puny little man!' shouted Antaeus. 'You hide behind your big guns and show the world what a coward you are!'

The ballistas stopped. Evadne's entire body tensed. That was a smart way to stop Hercules from firing his guns, but in a one-on-one fight, few could beat him, even giants. What was Antaeus thinking?

'You're not worth my time. Get out of the way,' she heard Hercules call back. From her crouched position, she could only see the side of the *Hybris*, the wheel blocking her view of the middle of the deck, where Hercules stood. She knew the hippocampus was tied up on the rear quarterdeck, where Asterion was.

'Fight me, little Hercules! My crew are stronger than yours and I am definitely stronger than you.'

Hercules laughed, long and loud.

'So the giants' legendary stupidity proves to be true!' he called. 'Have it your way.'

Evadne felt the whole *Hybris* jerk as Antaeus leaped through the hole in the net, onto the deck of Hercules's ship. The two brothers thudded onto the deck after him. Hercules didn't fight fairly, the giants must know that. Why would they bait him like this? Anxiety for Eryx was welling inside her. She didn't want them to fight. She didn't want Eryx anywhere near Hercules.

An internal war had been raging within Evadne all the way to Aquarius. Self-preservation, the need to be off the ship, was dominating her thoughts, but the small persistent voice insisting that Hercules must not win immortality wouldn't quieten down. Was she willing to risk her own life to stop him winning? Morally, she should at least try, for the sake of the thousands of other lives he may ruin in his endless future. But fear froze her thoughts, and crippled her ability to actually do anything. She wondered, from a selfish point of view, if she escaped and Hercules gained immortality, would he bother to come after her? Would she spend the rest of her life running from him? Or would he have far more exciting things to keep him busy, so that he forgot about her completely? Up until a few moments ago, she had

been formulating a plan to escape when they got to Poseidon's throne room, to try to disappear into the underwater city and take her chances. The selfish voice was
louder and had been winning. Who was she to go up
against somebody as powerful as Hercules?

But as she watched Eryx land on the deck of the
Hybris, she knew the choice had been made for her. She
couldn't let him die.

Antaeus and Hercules continued to taunt each other
while she crept as silently as she could to the front
hauler, before riding it all the way down to the cargo
deck. She was forming a new plan, fast. She'd found that
egg on Scorpio, and the tonic – the anapneo –inside it
was rightfully hers. It was time to show Hercules that he
hadn't beaten her. Not yet.

12

HEDONE

H edone couldn't decide how she felt about being relegated to the safety of Hercules's quarters. She understood that he might be distracted if he wasn't sure she was safe, but she felt utterly useless just sitting in his rooms, holding on when the ship lurched around. And the anxiety of not knowing if he was OK was killing her.

Eventually, fed up of pacing up and down the room, Hedone pulled open the door to the corridor. She had helped Theseus in every Trial, so surely she could be of some use to Hercules? But would he be mad with her for ignoring his instructions? What if she did distract him? She bit down on her bottom lip, then jumped in surprise as she saw a flash of movement at the end of the corridor. She stepped back into the room, pulling the door almost shut. Peeking through the gap, she watched as Evadne jogged quickly down the corridor and slipped into the galley. She was moving fast enough that Hedone suspected she was doing something she wasn't supposed to be.

Opening the door again, Hedone crept down the corridor, stepping silently into the galley. Evadne didn't notice her, as she was loading a bag with cans of food and jars of water.

'What are you doing?' she said.

Evadne whirled around, grabbing a kitchen knife from the countertop.

'There's no point trying to stop me!' she said with a calm that was belied by her shaking hand.

'Stop you doing what?' Hedone looked at the bag she was filling, and at her leather fighting clothes. 'Are you leaving?'

Evadne nodded.

'What happened to your hair?' Hedone asked, stepping closer. The sleek ponytail that Evadne normally wore was gone. Her blue hair had been cut short and hung jagged around her jaw.

'When Hercules asks, tell him you didn't see me,' Evadne said, still holding the knife up.

'Why are you leaving?' Evadne stared at her.

'You... You really don't know?'

'Know what?'

'How he treats me? If I stay here, he'll kill me, sooner or later.'

Hedone's face broke into a smile as she realised what was going on.

'Don't be silly. Of course he won't. You're just feeling insecure since I came on board. I'm sorry he made you give me your dresses, and I guess it's true life might be a little different for you on the *Hybris* now, but the life of a server for someone like Hercules is better than most in Olympus will ever get.'

Evadne let out a small, strangled laugh, and Hedone frowned.

'He cut my hair. He held a knife to my throat and he cut my ponytail off,' she said, a frantic edge to her voice.

'No. No, he wouldn't have done that,' Hedone said. The girl must be lying to her. Hercules had said she was cunning. But her hair... Nobody would have done that to themselves.

'He told me that if I tried to leave the ship, he would cut off something that didn't grow back,' Evadne said, her eyes now slightly wild. 'You don't need me here, Hedone. Just let me go and you'll never see me again.' She was still holding the knife up, and Hedone took a step backwards. An uncomfortable feeling was growing within her, the notion that something, somewhere, was terribly wrong that had plagued her for weeks bubbling up. Why *did* everyone want her to think Hercules was such a monster? Could they really all be wrong?

'Please,' Evadne said.

Hedone couldn't deny the fear that she saw in the girl's eyes was real. And she doubted Evadne was scared of her. Although she could use her powers of seduction to convince her to stay, and probably should if that was what Hercules wanted. But why? Why keep the girl here against her will?

'I will not stop you,' she said eventually. Evadne sagged, dropping the knife and returning to stuffing as much food as she could into the bag.

'Thank you,' she mumbled.

'Do you really believe he would hurt you?' Hedone asked her quietly, as Evadne slung the bag over her shoulder and turned back to face her.

'He already has. Many times.'

'No. Surely not,' Hedone said, shaking her head and frowning at the pity she now saw in Evadne's eyes.

'Be careful,' she said, then ran past her, into the corridor.

13

HERCULES

T he enormous idiot who had challenged him had no intention of fighting him, Hercules realised too late. Antaeus had taken off towards the rear quarterdeck as soon as Hercules had unsheathed *Keravnos*, and now he was stuck fighting the two brutish brothers while their captain tried to steal his prize.

'Asterion, guard that hippocampus with your life!' he roared as one of the brothers swung a fist at him. Hercules ducked, swiping his sword at the fat giant's wrist. The ensuing howl told him it had connected with flesh.

'I can't, Captain!' came the minotaur's strained reply. Hercules glanced sideways and saw the half-giant Eryx dancing around in front of Asterion, throwing jabs at him every time he tried to move towards the rear quarterdeck.

With a snarl, Hercules skidded under the legs of the bearded giant as he stamped a huge foot. Anger surged through him as the planks of the *Hybris* buckled beneath the brute's weight. He'd had enough of this. Who did these morons think they were, boarding *his* ship and trying to trick him? Did they think that because there were more of them they would win? Did they not understand what he was capable of?

He felt his muscles swell, his chest expand, his legs pump as he leaped to his feet. Continuing the same motion he broke into a run, heading away from the two giants. He heard their grunts of confusion, then the thud of their feet as they followed him.

When he reached the front mast he didn't slow down, instead jumping at the last second, forcing his strong thighs to continue to carry him up the pole. When he knew he was starting to slow down he spun, pushing himself hard off the mast, now six feet off the ground. As he started to fall back to the deck he flicked *Keravnos* out as far as his arm would reach, and felt the blade connect with the fat giant's throat. Hot blood spurted from the wound, and the giant collapsed immediately to his knees, the planks of the deck creaking and splitting as he landed.

'Albion!' The bearded giant's roar was so loud, the whole of the *Hybris* was shaking when Hercules landed a split second later. He didn't pause for breath, though, turning and powering towards the livid giant. His face was twisted in snarl of rage, and for a heartbeat, Hercules worried that he had underestimated him.

But the massive brute swung clumsily for him, and once again, Hercules was able to slide easily under his legs. This time, he raised *Keravnos* as he slid, swiping at the insides of the giant's thighs. The second brother howled, kicking out and clipping the lion-skin cloak and sending Hercules tumbling across the planks.

Hercules was righting himself when the giant's foot came towards him again, catching him square in the chest and sending him flying back towards the mast he'd just run up. Anger and pain sent adrenaline racing around his body, giving his thoughts a calm, battle-ready clarity. He got swiftly to his feet. He would enjoy this.

Keravnos glowed as the giant dropped his head and charged towards Hercules, who let him come. Instead of stepping aside, he widened his stance and lifted his sword to his chest so it jutted out, holding the hilt with both hands. He braced himself.

The giant hit him like a solid stone wall, shoulder dropped and chest level with Hercules's head. Although the lion-skin cloak took most of the blow, Hercules was only just able to hold his ground. But he did. And he held his sword straight too. There was a gurgling sound and the brute looked down at *Keravnos,* which had pierced deep into his gut.

Hercules lifted his leg and planted it on the giant, pushing him backwards off the sword. The giant clutched at his stomach as he stumbled backwards, then sank onto the planks beside his dead brother, blood flowing onto the broken deck. Hercules took a deep breath, a smile spreading across his face. Killing two giants that size should shut his father up for a while.

14

ERYX

Eryx's skin crawled as he heard Antaeus roar. He'd known Hercules was strong but... Regret and sadness swelled in him. Both brothers were dead, and the tangy stench of their blood filled his nostrils as he blocked the minotaur's relentless blows. He knew what his captain would do next. Antaeus was sure to abandon the plan. And if Hercules could destroy Albion and Bergion that quickly... Eryx had to help his captain.

He charged at Asterion with renewed determination, ducking and throwing a solid punch at the creature's gut. It connected, but not hard enough to wind him and the minotaur danced out of the way of the follow-up jab. The ship shuddered as Antaeus leaped down from the high quarterdeck and charged past them, and for a brief second, both Eryx and Asterion turned towards Hercules, their own fight suspended.

'Drop that cursed sword and fight me like a real man!' Antaeus thundered as he reached Hercules.

'You think it is my sword that makes me strong?'

laughed Hercules, and jammed *Keravnos* into the mast of the *Hybris*. 'I thought you were smarter than your brethren. I see I was wrong.'

Then the two of them were a blur, Antaeus's huge form lunging, punching and kicking at the smaller human as he darted this way and that, landing his own blows on the giant.

'Stop!' The minotaur's yell dragged Eryx's attention away from his captain and towards the back of the ship. Asterion was racing towards the high quarterdeck, where Busiris was just visible.

'Busiris! Leave the hippocampus! We need your help!' Eryx shouted as the minotaur bounded up the steps to the quarterdeck ahead of him. Eryx ran after him, taking them three at a time and skidding to a stop when he reached the top. Busiris was straining and heaving to get the struggling hippocampus up to the railings, where the *Orion*'s longboat was hovering on the other side.

The plan hadn't been to use the longboat, it had been to drag the creature straight through the hole in the net and onto the deck of the *Orion*. When had Busiris got the longboat? A sick, uneasy feeling spread through Eryx's gut as he made eye contact with the golden half-giant. He wasn't going to fight.

Asterion was only a few feet away now and Busiris heaved a final time, his muscles bulging as he lifted the tied-up animal high enough to throw it into the little boat. The hippocampus squealed as it landed with a thud. 'Busiris, no! You can't leave!' Eryx shouted as the minotaur roared.

Busiris threw him a last glance, a contemptuous smile

on his face as he jumped over the railings after the hippocampus, and then the longboat was zooming over them, racing back towards the *Orion*.' You cowardly bastard!' Eryx screamed, shaking his fist as the little boat zipped through the hole in the net. His stream of curses was cut short, though, as Asterion powered into him. He landed hard on his backside, and went skidding across the planks. His breath caught as he tipped off the edge of the quarterdeck, feeling nothing but air beneath him.

15

LYSSA

Lyssa gasped as she felt the ship break the surface of the water.

'Captain!'

'Lyssa!'

She could hear her name being called, both out loud and in her head, by everyone on the ship, but she couldn't answer them. She was still crouched on the planks under the fallen main sail, still pouring herself into the *Alastor*. She couldn't lose her ship. She couldn't.

The rest of the world had dimmed to nothing, the bond taking over all her other senses. She could feel the hole in the hull, water draining from it as they slowly lifted from the surface of the ocean. She could feel every broken plank and splintered panel of wood. Worst of all was the feeling of the toppled mast, the core of the ship split in two. It felt so wrong it made her feel sick. Waves of dizziness were engulfing her but she clung on, feeding the *Alastor* everything she had.

Suddenly light surrounded her, and as she looked up she saw Epizon towering over her as he ripped the sails back. He leaned down and she cried out as he scooped her up in his massive arms, breaking her connection with the wood of the ship. Convulsions immediately wracked her, and she tried to focus on Phyleus's voice somewhere in the distance as pain crippled her muscles.

'We're safe now, the ship's safe now. It's OK, Lyssa, you did it. We're all safe.'

We're all safe. They didn't know, they couldn't know, how broken the ship was. She tried to reach out for it, but she couldn't feel the reassuring presence, the hum of ancient power. Her stomach roiled and the light made her head pound when she tried to open her eyes. Waves of bone-deep exhaustion threatened to engulf her completely, and she was aware of how close she was to passing out.

'Abderos!' she yelled suddenly, feeling Epizon jump as he carried her across the deck. She began to struggle in his arms, looking around for the navigator, trying to orient herself and feeling her stomach heave as she did so. The cramping renewed itself with vigour and she couldn't stop herself from crying out in pain.

'I'm here, Cap,' Abderos replied in her mind, his voice shaky,

'Are we still above the water?' she gasped. Her body curled in on itself and she gripped her first mate's shirt as the seizures rocked her legs. Epizon held her tight.

'Yes.'

'How? Can you still feel the ship through the wheel?'

'Yes, Cap. But... it feels like you.'

A new wave of convulsions took over. The pain was so blinding that Lyssa lost her battle, and the darkness swallowed her up.

16

EVADNE

E vadne ran from the hauler onto the deck in time to
see Eryx skidding off the edge of the rear quarterdeck. He landed well, though, rolling as his shoulders hit
the planks first, and coming back up to his feet as Asterion leaped from the deck after him. Was the
hippocampus still up there? And where was the *Alastor*?
If Hercules won this Trial then he was as good as
immortal.

She scanned the rest of the deck, her mind racing as
she tried to make sense of the chaos. A cold, sick feeling
clamped around her chest as she took in the spreading
pool of blood under the bodies of Albion and Bergion.
Two full giants, and he had slaughtered them both in the
time she had been below decks. She could tell from their
wounds that they had both been felled by a sword, and
was surprised to see *Keravnos* sticking out of the main
mast.

Hercules and Antaeus were locked in a weaponless

wrestling match, crashing around the main deck of the *Hybris* in a lethal tumble. By all rights, the giant should win, given that he was twice the size of the human man and a legendary fighter, but Evadne feared for him. She knew what Hercules was capable of. There was no danger of her captain noticing her while he was so distracted, though, so she ran as lightly as she could down the steps from the front quarterdeck and along the railings, towards Eryx.

ONLY AS SHE ran past the hole in the net did she realise that the *Orion* was gone. She slowed down, squinting out into the sea, and could just make out the Zephyr in the blue beyond, chugging away towards the city of Aquarius. If Antaeus and Eryx were still here fighting, then... that must be Busiris. Hope swelled in Evadne. The throne room was in the city, so if the devious coward was heading that way, he must have the hippocampus. That meant one less thing for her to worry about.

A blood-curdling bellow halted her in her tracks and she turned to see Antaeus smashing into the deck of the *Hybris*. The broken and splintered planks gave out completely, and the giant's arms flailed wildly as his huge body sank into a mess of broken wood. The long planks began tipping and bending and Evadne gripped the railings as Hercules ran towards the giant.

'Captain!' she heard Eryx shout as Antaeus grappled to pull himself out of the destroyed deck, the broken wood tearing the bare skin of his stomach as he tried to heave himself free. Hercules was on him in an instant. He wrapped one massive arm around the giant's neck and Evadne's stomach churned as she guessed what was coming.

She dropped the pack from her shoulder, ripping it open and rummaging desperately for the crossbow she had stolen from the weapons room. She found it, and loaded a bolt into it with shaking hands. Hercules was wearing his lion skin, but Antaeus was thrashing enough that the cloak might slip. She just needed one good shot.

As she stood and levelled the weapon at her captain, Asterion suddenly flew past her, as though he'd been shot from a catapult, then Eryx was launching himself at Hercules.

Hercules didn't loosen his grip on Antaeus's neck, and the giant's face was now turning purple, but his other arm shot out as Eryx reached him. The blow caught Eryx square in the jaw and knocked him skidding across the deck towards Evadne. Hercules's eyes met hers, then flicked to the weapon in her hand. A slow, cruel smile spread across his face and fear paralysed her, her traitorous hand refusing to move. Antaeus was trying to pull himself out of the mangled deck with one arm, the other beating uselessly at Hercules.

'Are you going to shoot me, little girl?' Hercules called, wrapping his other arm around Antaeus's neck and squeezing. Antaeus gasped and choked. Out of the corner of her eye, Evadne saw Eryx stumbling to his feet.

'Let him go!' she shouted back, her voice shaking as much as her hands.

'Do you think he'll be a better lover than me? I suppose he is a big boy,' taunted Hercules. Antaeus's eyes were starting to bulge, and turn red at the edges.

'Let him go!' roared Eryx.

'I thought I'd enjoy killing you when I brought you on board, but I didn't know I'd want it this much,' Hercules said, his eyes still locked on hers.

'Eryx, leave, now,' Antaeus wheezed, and Hercules snapped his attention back to the giant. He swivelled around suddenly, keeping one arm round the giant's neck and yanking hard as he flipped himself over. There was a sickening crack and Evadne felt her legs go weak.

'No! No, no, no!' Eryx bellowed, as the life left Antaeus's eyes and he slumped forward. 'You fucking monster! You bastard!'

'Eryx, stop!' Evadne screamed as Hercules rolled to his feet. She fired instinctively, fear for Eryx overwhelming her own terror. The bolt thumped into Hercules's exposed shoulder. He stumbled backwards, tripping over Antaeus's body, a roar of anger bursting from him. Eryx was running for him as she screamed his name again.

'He told you to run, Eryx! Do as he told you! You can't help him now. Help me!' Eryx slowed down and turned to her as Hercules scrambled to his feet. 'Come with me, please!' She crammed every bit of fear and emotion she had into the sobbed plea, and relief flooded her as his legs began to move, running towards her now.

She grabbed the pack off the deck, and climbed up onto the railings. Eryx had nearly reached her, but

Hercules was only feet behind him, blood dripping down his chest and lethal fury in his expression.

'Jump!' Eryx yelled as he sprang at the railings. She took a massive breath and leaped from the *Hybris* into the ocean.

Hercules set sail form Crete and the first thing he did when he reached Libya was to

challenge Antaeus, who was famous across the world for his strength and skill at

wrestling. The giant had killed all those he fought, until Hercules slew him.

EXCERPT FROM

LIBRARY OF HISTORY BY DIODORUS SICULUS

Written 1 BC

Paraphrased by Eliza Raine

17

ERYX

Cold ocean engulfed Eryx and he kicked away from the *Hybris* as fast as he could, following Evadne as she swam up towards the surface. Fury such as he had never experienced before was hammering through his body. He would kill Hercules, if it was the last thing he ever did. Why was he following this girl like a coward? Why was he not there now, ending that evil man's life once and for all?

Antaeus's last croaked words rang through his mind. *Eryx, leave, now.* His captain had been good. He had been strong and solid and the only friend Eryx had ever really had. He hadn't deserved to die like that. He hadn't deserved to die at all.

Grief welled up inside Eryx, and he let out an involuntary roar of pain. Water filled his mouth and he thrashed around, panic overwhelming him. Then Evadne was gripping his arm, forcing liquid from a vial into his mouth. His body was desperate for air, swallowing water against his will, and then he tasted something so bitter he retched hard. To his surprise, his mouth filled with dry air. He gulped it down gratefully, chest heaving. What had she given him?

She watched him a second, then began swimming again, heading up towards the light. He kicked his legs, swimming after her. The image of Antaeus slumping forward as his neck snapped played over and over in his head as they swam, seeming to take an eternity to cover the distance. Had he done the right thing, following Evadne? She had tried to save Antaeus. He'd seen her, ready to take the shot before Hercules killed him. Busiris may have been right about her time on the *Hybris* being up, but he'd been wrong about her.

Painful truth forced its way through his aching skull. If Hercules had killed the full giants so easily, Eryx wouldn't have stood a chance on his own. *You can't help him now. Help me*, she'd said to him. She had known that would make him stop. She had saved his life.

He could help her. He could help her escape that monster.

A TENTATIVE CALM had taken hold of Eryx by the time they eventually broke the surface.

'I'm so sorry,' Evadne whispered, and he looked at her, treading water beside him, tears streaming from her bloodshot eyes, her wet hair stuck to her face.

'Did he hurt you?' he ground out. She shook her head.

'No.'

'How were we breathing? What was in that vial?'

'I stole the tonic that was inside the egg we won on Scorpio. It lets you breathe underwater.'

Eryx swivelled his body around in the water, scanning the expanse of blue. In the far distance he could see one of the hauler towers leading down to Aquarius. But a hundred feet to his right he could see the *Alastor*, hovering above the ocean. He began to kick towards it.

'Where are you going?' Evadne asked.

'To the *Alastor*.'

'They won't have us,' she answered. He stopped and turned to her, trying to hold onto the need for revenge, to squash the raging grief that threatened to overcome him.

'You mean they won't have you.' Pain flashed across Evadne's face. 'Athena told Captain Lyssa I was important in stopping Hercules. She'll take us.'

'You still want to fight him?'

'More than anything I've ever wanted anything in my life.'

18

EVADNE

E vadne swam after Eryx, her heart pounding. She was off the *Hybris*. And Eryx was alive. Her thoughts were flipping madly between a desire to run a million miles from Hercules and the Immortality Trials, and the desire to stay by Eryx's side and do whatever was in her power to stop Hercules from becoming immortal.

She burned with shame when the sound of Antaeus's neck snapping forced its way into her thoughts. How had that monster Hercules ever been her ally, her lover? And now she had to face his daughter. Fear pulsed through her, but she didn't believe Lyssa or the *Alastor*'s crew would kill her. Nor did she believe they would let her aboard, though.

She had enough tonic left to get to one of the hauler towers and the only reason she wasn't already heading that way was Eryx. If there was even the slightest chance Lyssa would let her stay with him, she had to try. Losing his captain was likely the worst thing that could possibly have happened to Eryx and her heart was breaking for him, the strength of her grief surprising even her. Tears hadn't stopped rolling down her face and it wasn't because of Antaeus's death. It was the anguish she'd seen on Eryx's face, the pain now etched into his features.

'There's something wrong with their ship,' he said from ahead of her. She looked up at the *Alastor*. He was right. The main mast was missing. Geryon had clearly done some damage. That explained why they were up above the surface, instead of fighting below the waves.

'That might help us,' she said. He turned to her with a frown. 'We can offer our assistance. I'm sure a half-giant would be invaluable in helping with repairs.'

He said nothing as he turned back to the ship.

'Hello! Captain Lyssa!' he bellowed. He kept shouting, until eventually they saw the dark-skinned form of her first mate appear at the railings.

'Eryx?'

'And Evadne, yes. We need your help. Antaeus is... dead.' He choked on the last word, and Evadne felt fresh tears forcing their way from her eyes.

Epizon said nothing for a long moment, then, 'I'll send the longboat.'

PHYLEUS PICKED them up five minutes later, and it wasn't until she was sitting in the tiny, battered little boat that Evadne realised how exhausted she was from their frantic swim. The muscular young man said nothing as they flew back up to the deck, just eyed her coldly. She avoided his gaze, instead trying to take in the damage to the *Alastor*.

'Captain Lyssa is indisposed just now. What do you need?' asked Epizon as they landed on the deck.

'We're here to offer our services to your crew,' said Eryx, clambering out of the longboat.

Epizon's eyebrows shot up.

'What?'

'Hercules killed my captain. He would have killed Evadne too. She saved my life.'

Yet more tears rolled down Evadne's face and she cursed them silently. Why would they not stop? How could she have any tears left by now?

Abderos rolled across the battered deck towards them, and the huge white centaur clopped closer as well.

'It looks like you could do with some help,' Eryx continued, gesturing at the fallen mast. It was obvious that they had started trying to remove the enormous, lifeless sail from the broken pole.

'Where's the *Orion*?' Phyleus asked.

'Busiris took it,' said Eryx. 'Along with the hippocampus. He'll probably reach the throne room soon.'

Everybody present visibly sagged with relief at his words.

'So Hercules won't win,' muttered Epizon.

'Not unless he catches the *Orion*. But Busiris had quite a head start.'

'Why aren't you trying to get back to your own ship, then?'

'Busiris is a cowardly traitor. He is as responsible for

Antaeus's death as that bastard Hercules,' Eryx spat. 'I'd rather fight alongside those who truly want that monster dead.'

'And you?' Phyleus said, looking at Evadne. 'Do you really want your own captain dead?' Everyone turned their gaze to her.

'He's not my captain any more,' she said quietly.

'It's true; she shot him,' said Eryx.

There was a short silence, and Evadne was sure they could all hear her pounding heart.

'We need to talk, as a crew,' said Epizon eventually, and gestured the others towards him.

'Athena said I was important,' Eryx reminded him, loudly. 'The satyr who saved my life on Libra knows that's true. Trust me, we all want the same thing now. We're on the same side.'

Epizon didn't answer him as the *Alastor* crew huddled together. Evadne looked at Eryx, her wet clothes heavy against her aching body. But Eryx didn't meet her eye as they stood, waiting.

After what seemed like an age, Epizon turned back to them.

'Fine. For now, you can stay on the ship. We'll decide how to test your loyalty before the next Trial,' he said. 'You'll have to stay in the cargo deck as we don't have any empty cabins, and it's the only place you'll fit.' He looked at Evadne, his dark eyes warm. 'You can use the bathing chamber in my rooms.'

'Thank you,' she whispered.

'You've got half an hour to clean yourselves up, then

you can help us with repairs,' he said to Eryx. The half-giant nodded.

'Thank you.'

'Don't thank us just yet. I wouldn't expect to stay here long once Lyssa's back in charge,' said Phyleus, looking at Evadne.

19

HEDONE

Hedone stumbled in the hauler as the *Hybris* lurched to one side. Her palms were sweating, and her anxiety was making her mouth dry. But she couldn't wait below decks any longer, listening to the roaring and crashing coming from above. She had to know that Hercules was OK. She could feel the ship moving now, fast.

As soon as the hauler doors slid open she ran onto the main deck, slowing down as she saw the carnage. Her hand flew to her mouth, the smell as much as the sight causing bile to rise in her throat. One of the black-skinned giants was lying in a pool of dark blood, his throat cut. His brother was a few feet away, a devastating wound in his belly. And ten feet from them, half submerged in the jagged, broken planks of the deck was Antaeus, his head lolling forward at a nauseating unnatural angle. They were all dead. Three full giants, dead. Fear for Hercules rocketed through her and she sprinted towards the front quarterdeck, skirting around the slick blood covering the wood.

'Hercules!' she gasped as she crested the top of the steps. He was in his red chair, staring out at Aquarius, which was growing larger as they sped towards it. He turned to her slowly, his face cold as ice. She saw blood, scarlet and fresh where his lion-skin cloak did not close around his chest. 'Hercules, are you all right?' She ran to him, dropping to her knees as she reached him, her hands flying to his body. 'Are you hurt? Who did this?'

'Evadne,' he growled.

Hedone's hands froze. Evadne? But... She had let the girl go. This was her fault. Tears filled her eyes as she met his. She saw such rage and anger in them that her courage failed. She couldn't tell him what she had done. Not now, when he was in the middle of battle. She would tell him later, she promised herself.

'Let me dress the wound,' she said, springing to her feet and starting to make for the hauler at the front of the ship.

'No. There's no time. We will catch that slimy king of Egypt with his stolen goods any minute,' he snarled, fixing his gaze back on the city. Hedone looked out into the blue and noticed the tiny form of the *Orion* in the distance. So they still had a chance of winning? Hope filled her, easing the gnawing dread.

'Where is Asterion?'

'Infirmary. He has a broken leg.'

'Did... Did *you* kill the giants?' she asked, quietly.

He turned his eyes towards her slowly. His grey irises looked darker than usual, like storm clouds. Something primal stirred in Hedone's gut and she almost took a step backwards.

'Yes, my love. They boarded my ship, stole my prize and called me a coward. I killed them.'

For a heartbeat, as she took in the words that dripped with menace, Hedone understood Evadne's fear. But as quickly as the clarity came, it was gone. How dare those brutes board the *Hybris* and try to kill its captain! Of course Hercules had defended himself. And who wouldn't be impressed by his prowess? How many men could achieve such a feat as killing three giants?

'And Evadne?'

'She escaped. With the little giant who broke Asterion's leg. Useless fucking minotaur,' he spat.

She flinched at his cursing.

'But we can still win?' she said, in as positive a tone as she could manage.

'Oh yes. We can still win,' Hercules snarled.

20

LYSSA

Lyssa groaned as light filtered into her vision. She tried to determine her surroundings as she lifted her pounding head to look around her. She was in the infirmary. Why? It all came back to her in a rush, and she pushed herself up quickly.

'The ship!'

'The *Alastor*'s OK, thanks to you,' said Phyleus and she swivelled her head around towards him. He was there, again, on his knees beside her low bed.

'You nearly killed yourself to save it, though,' she heard Len say, before he trotted into view. She blinked at him, her headache receding quickly.

'I... I don't remember all of it,' she said, trying to recall her desperate fight to keep the *Alastor* above the water, to stop it from breaking and sinking. To save it from dying.

'You gave the ship everything. As in all of your power,' Phyleus said quietly.

'What? Is that even possible?' she whirled back to face Len.

The little satyr shrugged. 'Looks like it.'

Lyssa tentatively reached out to the ship with her mind, hoping for the faint sense of reassurance she always got from it. A blast of power, strong and fierce and restless answered her, and she gasped aloud.

'How...? I'm not even touching the mast!'

'It's you, Lyssa, it's your power. It's part of the ship now.'

'Forever?'

'I've no idea. But it's your power that's keeping the *Alastor* together without a mast or sail right now,' said Len. Lyssa stared at him. 'Speaking of which, I need to go and help the others with stitching the sails. Call me if you need me. Although... I doubt you will,' he said, with an uneasy look at her he trotted out of the small room.

'I can only pray that one day you feel as strongly about me as you do about this ship,' said Phyleus, a moment after Len had left. She raised her eyebrows at him. 'You... You were gone, Lyssa. You gave yourself up for the ship.'

Lyssa screwed her eyes shut. She didn't understand what he was saying, not fully. When she opened them again and looked at him, his eyes were narrow and his mouth a tight line. 'What were you thinking?'

'I wasn't thinking anything! I just knew that I had to save the *Alastor*,' she snapped. 'And it can't have been that bad. I actually feel fine.' She swung her legs out of the bed to prove her point. Phyleus let out a long breath.

'You feel fine because Len gave you ambrosia,' he said.

Her mouth fell open. 'What? Why?'

'Lyssa, you're not listening to me! You were practically dead! You gave the *Alastor everything*! That's not an exaggeration. It's a bloody miracle you're alive!' Phyleus was on his feet, shouting at her, his arms waving wildly.

'But...' she stammered, staring at him.

'Gods, Lyssa, I thought I'd lost you,' he said, and the intensity, the love, in his eyes made her breath catch.

'Phyleus, I'm sorry,' she whispered, not knowing what else to say. He dropped to his knees and then he was kissing her like his life depended on it. She kissed him back, trying to prove to him that she was here, she was OK, she was with him. Trying to ease his pain.

'Lyssa, please, please don't ever do that again,' he said as he broke the kiss, holding her face in his hands. 'Please.'

'OK,' she breathed, still not entirely sure what she'd done. She leaned forward to kiss him again, but there was a flash of white light and they weren't in the infirmary anymore.

She scrabbled to her feet as she looked around. They were in a throne room. A stunning throne room. Its marble floor was the palest blue, like the sea foam on crashing waves. There were no walls, just riveted columns holding up the roof, and she could see the city of Aquarius glowing in the background. The temple ceiling was painted with an exquisite image of a water garden, with strange creatures dancing amongst the beautiful plants. At the end of the room, on a raised dais, stood a marble throne shaped like a tidal wave, the stone curving perfectly to form a seat. And on that seat was Poseidon.

He stood up, slowly. Lyssa bowed immediately, aware of Phyleus doing the same next to her. She looked quickly from side to side while her head was down, taking in the other crew members. Her skin tingled and fizzed as she saw Hercules standing far to her right, his lion-skin cloak stained with blood and fury etched into his face.

'Heroes,' said the god. Lyssa straightened up, hope surging through her. If Hercules looked that angry... She scanned the faces around her, looking for Antaeus and praying she would see a triumphant expression on the giant's broad face. But Antaeus wasn't there.

'The *Orion* was first to return here with one of Geryon's hippocampus. They are the winners,' Poseidon boomed. Busiris stepped forward and gave a low, exaggerated bow.

'Thank you, divine one,' he purred. Lyssa looked around for the rest of the *Orion* crew, frowning. What was going on?

'Hercules,' said Poseidon, turning towards him. Hercules's face tightened, and it was clear that he was barely maintaining his calm mask. 'I have no objection to you killing members of the other crews, but I object deeply to the slaughter of Geryon's cattle. I am technically not able to punish you, as there are no rules governing these Trials. But know this. You have personally insulted a valued citizen of Aquarius and I am offended.'

The god's voice was so low it was barely audible, yet his words were like blades piercing Lyssa's ears, sharp and terrifying. Fear, deep and involuntary, shivered through her. But Hercules deserved the wrath of an Olympian, she thought, viciously.

Poseidon's words filtered through her fuzzy brain. The god said Hercules had killed members of another crew. She spun around, looking for the other giants, surprised but relieved to see Eryx behind her. She couldn't help liking the striking-looking boxer. He was standing next to Epizon and Evadne, though. Lyssa screwed up her face in confusion. Why were they standing with her crew?

'Go. Your next Trial will be announced in two days,' said Poseidon abruptly.

There was a flash of white and they were back on the deck of the *Alastor*. Lyssa closed her eyes and took a deep breath, trying to force her thoughts to line up.

'Epizon,' she said loudly. 'Epizon, if I turn around and see that snake from the *Hybris* on my ship, you're losing your position as first mate.'

Silence met her statement. Her stomach lurched as she turned around, and looked straight into Evadne's eyes.

ZEUS

THE IMMORTALITY TRIALS

TRIAL ELEVEN

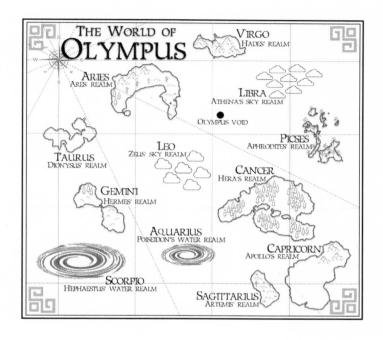

THE WORLD OF
OLYMPUS

VIRGO
HADES' REALM

ARIES
ARES' REALM

LIBRA
ATHENA'S SKY REALM

OLYMPUS VOID

PICSES
APHRODITES' REALM

LEO
ZEUS' SKY REALM

TAURUS
DIONYSUS' REALM

CANCER
HERA'S REALM

GEMINI
HERMES' REALM

AQUARIUS
POSEIDON'S WATER REALM

CAPRICORN
APOLLO'S REALM

SCORPIO
HEPHAESTUS' WATER REALM

SAGITTARIUS
ARTEMIS' REALM

1

LYSSA

Lyssa stared at Evadne, her fists clenching hard at her sides. The girl flinched, dropping her gaze to the planks.

'Captain Lyssa, we're grateful for your sanctuary,' said Eryx, stepping forward and bowing his head. 'Hercules killed my captain and I will not rest until he is dead. I think fighting alongside you is the best chance I have.'

Lyssa's pounding Rage faltered a little at the big man's words. His pain was barely concealed on his gaunt, tight face.

'I'm sorry about Antaeus,' she said to him. 'He was a good man, and I'd have been happy to see him win. But she needs to be off my ship. Now.'

'But Captain, she attacked Hercules!' said Abderos. Lyssa turned to her navigator and he rolled backwards at the fury that must have been showing on her face. 'Just talk to her, Cap,' he mumbled.

'Captain Lyssa, I'm sorry.' Evadne's voice drew Lyssa's attention back to her. She was rubbing her hands together nervously, and Lyssa realised her usual high ponytail had been cut short and ragged, so that her blue hair was now hanging in front of her face. 'I'm sorry for what happened to you and your family and I'm sorry I ever believed in that man. And I'm sorry for any harm I intended you or you crew. I want Hercules dead.' She raised her head, and her expression was hard and fierce. 'I will do whatever it takes to help you end this.'

'I'd be a fool to trust you, Evadne,' Lyssa spat.

'The whole of Olympus saw her shoot him. You saw the blood yourself,' said Epizon quietly. 'She can help us, Captain. She's been on the *Hybris*, she knows how he thinks.'

'And I can give you what's left of this,' Evadne said, reaching into her pocket. 'If I wanted to leave, I could sell this for a fortune. Without it I only have the clothes on my back.' She held out a small glass vial. Lyssa stepped forward and took it suspiciously.

'Len?' she called. The satyr trotted up and took the bottle from her.

'Looks like anapneo, Captain.'

Evadne nodded. 'It's how we escaped from the *Hybris*.'

'And you all think this is a good idea?' Lyssa looked at each of her crew in turn. Most of them nodded, Abderos and Epizon enthusiastically, Len and Nestor less so. Her gaze settled on Phyleus.

'If she did shoot him, he'll kill her without our protection,' he said in her mind.

'Not my problem,' she answered.

'I think Eryx may leave with her if you kick her off the

ship. And he could be really useful. Plus Athena said he was important.'

Lyssa let out a long breath.

'Fine,' she said aloud. Eryx sagged and a solitary tear slid down Evadne's cheek.

'Thank you,' she whispered. Lyssa did not reply, but addressed her crew again.

'Everyone, back to repairing the ship. Let's make the most of this break. As soon as the *Alastor* is fixed we'll head towards Leo and Virgo: the next Trial has to be on one of them and they're pretty close to each other. Abderos, galley duty, please, I'm starving. Make enough stew for fifteen if you can manage it.'

'Aye, Cap,' he said, and rolled off. Everyone else headed towards the massive sail laid out on the main deck.

'Um, do I still have a job?' said Epizon, from behind her.

She turned and rolled her eyes. 'Until she stabs us all in our sleep, sure, you can keep your job,' she muttered.

'Thank you, Captain. Len said you saved the ship but he was sketchy on the details. And the *Alastor* feels different. What happened?'

'I'm not really sure. But it doesn't matter now, we're both OK. What damage have we taken?' Lyssa felt awkward sidestepping the question, but she didn't know how to tell him that she had apparently practically killed herself. She hadn't even known what she was doing, just that the ship couldn't die. She felt a surge of something under her skin and shook it off. She'd work out what her actions had cost her later.

'We have a large hole in the hull, and obviously the main mast is broken in two. The ripped sails are coming along well, but we may need your strength when we try to right the mast.'

'Good,' she said and strode towards the hauler. 'I'm going for a bath, I'll be back in an hour.'

'Before you go...' He trailed off and she turned back to him. 'A lot of light was let into the cargo deck when the hull was breached.'

Lyssa sighed. She knew what that meant.

'So Tenebrae is all topped up?'

'I think so. She's... She's talking to me,' Epizon said.

Lyssa's eyebrows shot up.

'Talking to you? What do you mean?'

'Well, I think it's her way of talking. She shows me images, mostly of things I'm familiar with. She's been showing me memories of my mother I didn't know I still had.'

'Epizon, I'm sorry,' Lyssa said, sadness filling her.

'It's fine,' he said, shaking his head. 'Actually, it's nice. And I'm sure it's Tenebrae causing the images. Every now and again something comes through that's not one of my memories.'

'Like what?'

'Well, they're hard to describe. Just flashes that come and go. But she definitely lived underwater. And she loves light, but I'm not sure she actually needs it to live.'

'Do you know what she eats yet?'

'No. But I'm positive that it's her who doesn't want to go to Virgo.'

Lyssa nodded. She had suspected as much.

'OK. Maybe we can take the longboat, leave her as far from the realm as we can?'

Relief washed over Epizon's face.

'That would be great, Captain.'

'Do you think she's dangerous?' The fact that she could hide from a god proved she was, but Lyssa wanted to know what Epizon thought. The idea of the weird creature inside her best friend's head was not sitting well at all.

'Yes. But not to us.'

That was a good answer, Lyssa thought.

2

EVADNE

E vadne watched the little satyr trot off with the anapneo, heart still hammering in her chest. Had she just made a massive mistake? That vial was her ticket to freedom. They may have used most of it, but there was enough to sell to get her passage home. She watched Eryx lurch past her, to the splintered mast in the middle of the deck. Nestor and Phyleus were laying out the sails, finding the tears and pointing them out to the satyr, who began stitching them back up.

'Eryx, can you help us with the hull, please?' called Epizon. Eryx nodded and followed him to the massive cargo hauler. Evadne's stomach flipped as she realised she was now standing on her own.

'What can I do?' she asked loudly, speaking to nobody in particular. The lost feeling was threatening to swamp her.

'Can you sew?' Phyleus asked her.

'Yes.'

'Good. Come help Len.' She obliged, quickly. Doing something was definitely better than doing nothing, even if she would rather have been wherever Eryx was.

The satyr gave her some coarse thread and a thick needle and she set to work on the nearest rip.

'I'm the ship's medic,' Len said gruffly, after ten minutes of working in silence.

'I'm... I was a gunner.'

'Huh. No guns here,' he answered.

'Good,' she shuddered, remembering the crossbow bolt thunking into Hippolyta's stomach.

'Can you climb?' asked Phyleus, appearing around the broken stump of the mast.

'Yeah. Pretty well, actually,' she said, standing up.

'Great. You can help me re-tie the top sail on the front mast.'

She followed him to the base of the shorter, intact, mast and looked up. The top sail was drooping unnaturally. 'Can you climb out to the right boom and check all the knot-work?' he said.

'Sure,' she replied.

Phyleus nodded, then pulled his shirt off and she blinked. He was way more muscular than she had realised. She supposed being dwarfed by men like Epizon, Hercules and Eryx must had made him look smaller than he really was. He hooked his arms around the pole and began to climb up the mast easily, and she pushed her hair back from her face, then hurried after him.

.   .   .

THEY WORKED on the sails for another hour, then Lyssa insisted everyone stop for food. The galley was too small for them all to eat there, so Evadne helped bring up bowls of stew to the main deck, where they sat around on the tired old planks. Conversation was awkward and stilted, but not painfully so. Slowly, Evadne's racing heart was calming down.

'I don't know how we can fuse the mast back together, Captain,' Len was saying to Lyssa. 'It's not like the holes we fix, we can't just nail new wood down. And we don't have anything on board strong enough to hold a mast that size up.'

Lyssa's face was pinched and worried.

'Can we tie it?'

'Maybe. If we had bigger staples we might be able to do something more robust.'

'Staples?' Lyssa flinched.

'Cap, the ship's not going to be good as new. It's only 'cos of you it's still flying at all,' Len said gently. 'We'll have to try something temporary until we can get more materials.'

She sighed.

'Do you have any favours you can call in? Some help from Athena, perhaps?' Evadne asked tentatively. Lyssa snorted.

'I know that's how it works on the *Hybris*, but we've had no help at all from our patron goddess. In fact the only time we've seen her was when she asked about...' Lyssa trailed off and looked at Epizon. 'Ep, do you think Tenebrae could help us?'

The big man raised his eyebrows and tilted his head.

'I could try and ask her,' he said slowly.

'Who's Tenebrae?' asked Eryx, the spoon he was holding looking tiny in his big hands.

'You probably noticed the big tank in the cargo deck?' asked Abderos. Eryx nodded. 'The thing in it. She's called Tenebrae.'

Interest surged through Evadne.

'What is she?' she asked.

'We don't know, and her presence here is a secret. If you tell anyone she's here, I'll throw you off the ship from a height you won't survive,' said Lyssa, shooting her a look.

'I've seen her chuck bodies overboard. It's as alarming as it sounds,' said Phyleus.

'OK,' Evadne said, burning to go and look at this thing in a tank.

'Would we need to bring her up here again?' asked Abderos anxiously. 'It's just, it wasn't very nice last time.'

'I dunno, Epizon is the only one she—' Lyssa's answer was cut off abruptly as the fallen mast lifted suddenly from the planks of the deck. Nestor shouted, leaping sideways out of its path and Phyleus yelped, dropping to the ground as it whizzed over his head.

'Sorry, Captain! I just asked her, I didn't think it would work!' Epizon called out.

Evadne's mouth fell open as the mast straightened vertically, high above them, then dropped onto the severed stump. There was a searing flash of red light and as it died away Lyssa leaped to her feet. She ran to the mast, and Evadne pushed herself up quickly to follow. They all crowded around, gaping.

'Well. Would you look at that,' said Len, and let out a long whistle as Lyssa reached out and tentatively touched the wooden mast, perfectly fused back together. 'As good as new.'

3

LYSSA

Once the main mast was back up, it took no time at all to hang the repaired sails. They didn't sit quite right, pinched and pulling where the rips had been sewn up, but the feeling that rushed through Lyssa's body when they secured the last one and the light shimmered across it, told her the repairs were enough. She wanted to find out if she could pour her power into the ship from anywhere, not just right next to the mast with her hands on the wood, now that her connection was so strong; but it seemed too soon to push the ship, and the pulsing life she could feel thrumming from the sails was enough for now.

'It's all yours, Ab. Let's see if we can get halfway between Leo and Virgo.'

'Aye, Cap.'

She felt the *Alastor* move beneath her, hope and that blissful feeling of freedom easing her mind for a moment. But the feeling was short-lived. They had over a day until the next announcement. And she had some serious thinking to do in that time.

Although she knew she needed to untangle her thoughts about Evadne and Eryx coming on board, about Tenebrae and how they were going to keep her away from Virgo, about how they were going to stop Hercules and win the next Trial, her brain kept pulling her back to the same thing: *I can only pray that one day you feel as strongly about me as you do about this ship*. Phyleus's words were playing over and over in her head. She couldn't ignore them any longer.

She told everyone to get some rest and went quickly to her own cabin, where she threw herself down on her bed with a sigh. Phyleus deserved better than her scattered, unsure, lust-fuelled kisses. There was no point trying to avoid it, she needed to make some decisions. She sat up and closed her eyes, trying to picture herself with Phyleus. She remembered the feeling of the *Alastor* slipping away under hands, the unbearable fear and loss she felt at losing the ship, losing her freedom, losing part of her own life. Were those really her own feelings? Or was her bond with the ship so deep that she had felt its fear as her own?

Her life had begun anew when she bought the *Alastor*. Before that, the thought of owning a ship and escaping on it had been a dream, a shining beacon, something to cling to throughout her darkest times. And when she finally stood on the deck with Epizon for the first time it had been everything she had wanted and more. When they took Len and Abderos on board she had felt like she had a family again, something she had never thought possible. The *Alastor* wasn't just her home, her livelihood, her way out. It enabled and supported her whole life, her crew's lives. It was a part of her.

She reached out to it, gently. The pulsing power was different now, light and energetic, dancing and free. They were sailing through the skies of Olympus, just as the ship wanted to. It was happy, she realised, as a broad smile spread across her face involuntarily.

If she'd lost Phyleus, would she have done the same thing? She thought about Abderos, torn and bloody at the feet of the monstrous horses, and knew without hesitation that she would give herself up for him. She thought of Epizon bloody and lifeless in the ocean, and knew the same was true for him too. But they were like brothers to her; she already knew that she loved them. Did that make Phyleus right when he had said that she was already sharing herself with others, that being with him would be no different? But it *would* be different. If she let him in, let those fierce sparks of lust turn to love... What if she lost him? A vision of her mother, bloody and screaming as she tried to shield Lyssa's little brother, filled her mind.

Hot tears burned at the back of her eyes as stark realisation hit her. She knew what her problem was, why she wouldn't let him in. She didn't know how she would ever recover if she lost someone she loved that intensely again.

'CAP, ABOUT THE AMBROSIA.' Len's voice in her head punctured her spiralling sadness. 'You need to let me know if you feel weird at any point. Weak or dizzy.'

'Oh, right, um...' She shook her head, taking a deep breath. 'I don't feel weak at all.'

'You won't yet. You should feel like a million drachmas. But tell me immediately if you start getting crippling headaches tomorrow.'

She screwed her face up.

'Right. Will do. While we're talking, do you have any ideas about Epizon's connection with Tenebrae? Should we be worried, from a medical point of view?'

'Even if I was worried, there's nothing you or I can do about it,' he said, matter-of-factly. 'If she's in his head, we can't get her out.'

'Right,' Lyssa answered, her shoulders drooping. She supposed it was true, although that didn't make her feel any better.

'Sleep well, Cap.'

SHE TRIED TO SLEEP, but her racing mind wouldn't allow it. As the light dimmed outside the portholes she decided to go up to the top deck, in the hope that everyone else would have retired to their rooms. Deep violet clouds corkscrewed over her head as she stepped out of the hauler, and a warm breeze whipped at her hair. They were moving fast, and she took a long breath, savouring the feeling of motion.

'Hi,' said a quiet voice. She turned to see Phyleus leaning against the railings. Her stomach flipped uneasily.

'Hi,' she said, walking over to him slowly.

'Trouble sleeping?' She nodded.

'You too?' He looked at her, silent for a long moment.

'I don't think I'll sleep for some time,' he said eventually. She frowned at him.

'Why?'

'You don't get it, do you?' His voice was filled with frustration and she stepped closer to him as he pushed his hands through his hair angrily. 'Lyssa, I feel it when somebody is about to die. Today I knew for certain that the woman I love was going to die.'

Understanding washed through Lyssa as she looked at his wild, red-rimmed eyes, quickly followed by guilt and a feeling she couldn't quite identify.

'Oh, Phyleus, I didn't think... I'm sorry,' she said, moving close to him, her heart hammering.

'Why? Why did you do it?' he asked, hoarsely.

'I didn't make a conscious decision to die, Phyleus. I just let my power take over. The *Alastor* is a part of me, it's not just wood and metal.'

He turned back to the clouds, taking a deep breath.

'I know that. I just...' He trailed off.

'Phyleus, I'd do the same for you. I swear it.'

He turned back to her.

'You would?'

'Yes. I've been thinking. And I know why we can't be together.' He stilled and Lyssa swallowed. 'Losing my mother and brother nearly destroyed me. I don't think I ever properly got over it, even now. I mean, I'm hardly normal. Hercules is the most dangerous man in Olympus, and there's nobody he wants to hurt more than me. Which means he will try to kill you. If he wins the Immortality Trials and we survive, then he will hunt us.

Forever. And if he killed you to get to me... I don't think I could recover. I can't go back to that place again.' She could feel the burning tears roll down her cheeks as she spoke, but for once she didn't care that someone could see her crying. She wanted him to know how hard this was for her.

'I would run with you. He'll hunt you with or without me, and I would run with you.'

'I can't watch you die.'

He said nothing and it was all Lyssa could do to keep sobs from escaping her throat.

'This ship and its crew needs you,' he said eventually. 'I understand.'

Lyssa was sure she could actually feel pain in her chest as he said the words. Had she wanted him to fight, to convince her otherwise?

'I'm not leaving your side until after the Trials, though. If he kills me before the end, then—'

'Then chances are he'll kill me too.' She finished his sentence quickly. 'I'm sorry,' she whispered, then whirled around, half running to the hauler.

4

ERYX

Eryx stared at the thing in the tank as it swished its iridescent tail through the thick, unmoving liquid. It stared back, eyes huge and unblinking.

'What do you think it is?' asked Evadne.

'No idea.' He shrugged, and turned away. Epizon had opened a crate and hauled out piles of blankets, and now Eryx set about arranging them into a pile that vaguely resembled a bed. 'Where do you want to sleep?' he asked Evadne gruffly. 'I don't think they're going to give you a cabin, so I guess you're down here too.'

She pulled her gaze from Tenebrae and looked at him.

'I'll... I'll sleep as close to you as I can,' she said quietly.

Nerves skittered through his exhausted body and he looked away. Dragging some blankets from the nest he'd built, he started towards the nearest pile of crates. 'Behind here?' he asked. 'You'd have a bit of privacy.'

'Eryx...' her cheeks reddened. 'That looks pretty

comfy.' She pointed at his heap of sheets. She wanted his bed? Or she wanted to share his bed...

'I, er, I...' he stuttered.

'I'm not suggesting anything untoward,' she said, rolling her eyes. Eryx couldn't help the flash of relief he felt at the glimpse of the sarcastic, irritable Evadne he knew. 'It would just be a bit of comfort, knowing you're there. I'm not exactly popular on this ship.'

'They'll come round,' he said softly. 'They're good people.'

Evadne nodded. Neither of them spoke for a moment, then Eryx shrugged and carried the blankets back to his nest.

'Fine,' he said, and flopped down into the pile. He tried to ignore his racing heart as she walked towards him. She lifted her shirt a little to undo the trousers she was wearing and he rolled over quickly.

'Don't worry, I'll keep the shirt on,' she said, a slight chuckle in her voice. He didn't answer.

ERYX KNEW he had to sleep, but he'd been putting it off since he'd come aboard the *Alastor* for a reason. As long as he was keeping busy, achieving something, being useful, his mind was occupied. But now, as he lay in the semi-darkness, the emotions he'd barely been able to suppress since watching Antaeus slump forward, dead, began running rampant. Memories crashed over him in waves: all the times his captain had fought alongside him over the years, helped him out of situations where he couldn't win, pushed him in the right direction when his simple mind couldn't work out which way to go. Antaeus had called him brother because he'd felt it too. The connection they'd had was a friendship that ran deeper than blood.

Eryx didn't cry. He was a fighter with giants' blood, and tears had been trained out of him as a small child. But the human half of him was breaking. He couldn't help the heave of his shoulders as a dry sob racked him, unbidden.

A warm touch on his shoulder startled him, then he felt more warmth as Evadne pressed herself again his back. He felt her arm wrap around his middle, tight and solid. Mortification at her seeing him so weak warred with a surge of gratitude and a desperate need to not be alone. Fresh emotion rolled through him and then tears did come, hot and real and alien. Evadne said nothing, for which he was even more grateful, but her grip around him didn't loosen, and her message was clear. He had lost his best friend, his brother, his captain. But he wasn't alone.

5

HERCULES

Hercules launched what must have been his fifth glass across the living room. It smashed against the wooden planks of the wall with a pitiful tinkling sound and he felt Hedone jump beside him. She was curled up on the plush couch and had been dozing but he couldn't sleep. Every time he tried, Evadne's face would fill his mind and fresh fury would roll through his body.

'How dare she!' he roared, and Hedone pushed herself up quickly.

'Calm yourself, my love,' she said soothingly.

'She was nothing until I found her!' He banged his fist on the arm of the chair and it shuddered beneath them.

'And she'll be nothing once again.' Hedone ran her hand down his stubbled cheek. It felt good, her touch like warm silk. 'You cannot change what has happened. But you can still win the Trials.'

He closed his eyes, drinking in her words. They were true. He could easily still win.

'I will kill that gold giant,' he muttered, leaning back against the chair as Hedone's touch moved down his neck, towards his bare chest.

'Just concentrate on winning,' she murmured, and leaned in, planting kisses in the wake of her fingers.

'This wasn't how I pictured our first full day together, you know,' he said.

'I know. Once this is over, we can rest. Spend long, lazy days doing whatever we wish. We'll live in a mansion, with beautiful gardens, and music and feasts.'

Hercules let himself be sucked in by the vision she began to paint, her descriptions of the gardens, the pool, the bed, the food and drink, all vivid and delicious. He pulled her onto his lap, his tension easing when her heard her little giggle, saw the love in her eyes as she sat astride him.

'And you are happy to live with me on Leo?' he asked her.

'Of course. There is no place for me on Pisces any more.' He searched for regret or sadness in her words, but could find none.

They spent the rest of the evening talking, Hedone planning their future home while he drank wine and listened. He would give her everything she wanted, he vowed silently. And he would have infinity to deliver it.

THE NEXT MORNING he sat at the fire dish, waiting for the Trial announcement with restless anticipation. Ati the hairless cat was in a tight ball on Hedone's lap as she sat, cross-legged on the planks. Asterion stood silently behind him. Everybody knew what was at stake now, what a win for them would mean. His chest had healed fast, the bolt hadn't gone too deep, and Hercules felt ready to fight. He *needed* to fight.

'Good day, Olympus!' The blond announcer cried as soon as his image solidified in the flames. 'Well, well, well. Weren't we given a treat! Who would have thought everyone but the king of Egypt would be wiped off the *Orion* in that last Trial? And Hercules has made an enemy of Poseidon himself! That's two Olympians who hate you now, big man! You might want to watch that...' He gave an exaggerated wink and Hercules felt his hands tighten into fists as his lip curled. He'd show them all. All he needed to do was become immortal, and he would have eternity to show them exactly what he was made of. Starting with this pathetic pretty boy. 'Now, here to announce the next Trial...' The announcer faded from view, and Zeus's handsome face shimmered into focus.

'Heroes,' he said, without a smile. 'You have all performed admirably so far. My Trial will test you, though. Hidden in my realm is an island on which grows a very special tree, laden with golden apples. I want you to obtain one. They are guarded by one of my most precious pets, Ladon. I have no objection to you trying to kill him, as I believe that would be near impossible, and my respect for you would outweigh my loss if you managed it. However,' he boomed, and purple lightning crackled across his grey irises, 'the island is inhabited by the Hesperides. These women are under my protection, and if any of you lay a finger on them, you will suffer my wrath.' Hedone shrank back from the flame dish, her eyes wide as Zeus's form seemed to grow in the image. 'And living an immortal life with my wrath would not be pleasant. Just ask Prometheus.' Energy and power poured from the god, tangible even through the flame dish. Hercules suppressed his awe, pinching his lips tight together. 'Good luck,' Zeus said, then vanished.

Hercules turned to Asterion.

'Head for the outer islands on the north side of Leo. I know all the ones in the south well and I've never heard of this Ladon before.'

'Yes, Captain.'

'And we go as fast as possible.'

'Yes, Captain.'

As an eleventh labour Hercules was ordered to fetch golden apples from the Hesperides. They were guarded by an immortal dragon which spoke with many voices... Hercules seized Nereus, and the god shifted through many shapes, but Hercules would not release him until he had given him the whereabouts of the Hesperides and the golden apples.

EXCERPT FROM

THE LIBRARY BY APOLLODORUS

Written 300–100 BC

Paraphrased by Eliza Raine

6

LYSSA

'Hercules could have the home advantage on Leo,' said Nestor seriously as the whole crew of the *Alastor*, plus Eryx and Evadne, stared at the fading image of Zeus in the flame dish.

'Technically, it's my home too,' said Lyssa, with a small scowl. 'And there's no way that island is in the south. I know those islands. We head north.'

'Got it, Cap,' said Abderos, and she felt the ship shift slightly.

'Captain, it is imperative that he does not win this one. I know the gold giant won the last Trial, but I feel it is unlikely he will be able to win another by himself. The responsibility will now be on us.' Nestor's tone was grave and it wasn't helping Lyssa's skittering nerves.

'I'm well aware of that, Nestor,' she said as patiently as she could manage. After her conversation with Phyleus she had spent hours trying to focus herself, trying to block out any feelings that were unimportant and turn herself into the tool of revenge she had been starting to feel like after the first few Trials.

But it wasn't working. She felt restless and jittery, like she was teetering on a knife edge and nothing could ground her. She'd tried talking to Epizon, but he just told her she was making a huge mistake in walking away from Phyleus, which wasn't what she had wanted to hear. Epizon didn't understand what she was telling him, couldn't see the fear that would consume her, stop her from facing Hercules, if she had something that great to lose. *If she had love to lose.*

'How are we going to tackle this one, Captain?' Len asked her. She looked down at him, then cast a sideways glance at Evadne and Eryx.

'I don't know. Anybody know what Zeus's pet, Ladon, is?'

Len shook his head and she looked around at her crew until Evadne said, 'I do.'

'Really?' Abderos asked her.

'Yes. He's a dragon,' she answered, finding Lyssa's eyes. 'I don't know where the island is and I haven't heard of the golden apples, but I've read a number of accounts of Ladon guarding the beautiful Hesperides. They are forest nymphs that Zeus created especially for his own amusement centuries ago.'

'No kidding?' Len said, his furry eyebrows raised.

'Captain, if I may...' Evadne looked at her and Lyssa searched her face, her instinctive distrust of the girl trying to take over. *She shot him,* Lyssa thought. *She discovered what an abusive asshole Hercules was the hard way and now she's a good guy*, she told herself.

'Go on,' she said.

'It will be incredibly difficult to get past Ladon, and Hercules will relish the fight. I would consider trying a different tactic to get one of these apples. I would see if you can get the Hesperides to give you one.'

Lyssa stared at her.

'If we try that and fail, Hercules will have a clear path to victory,' she said eventually.

'He's more likely to defeat the dragon than you are,' said Evadne. 'I mean no offence, but he is stronger than you, he has *Keravnos* and Asterion is a good fighter.'

'Don't underestimate my crew, Evadne. Nestor is a fierce fighter too, and Phyleus and Epizon can distract the dragon from the longboat.'

'And risk their lives doing so. If you go directly to the Hesperides, you may convince them to help you with no bloodshed at all.'

'You just said that they're creations of Zeus! Why would they help me when Hercules is Zeus's hero?'

'You have Zeus's ichor in your veins. And they are women, capable of love. They may rally to your cause if you explain the situation.'

'What, that my rival is a murderous lunatic who killed my family and really shouldn't live forever?' Lyssa snorted but Evadne shrugged.

'Yes.'

'You know, Cap, it's really not a bad idea,' said Len.

'I agree,' said Epizon.

'I also agree, though I would suggest an amendment,' said Nestor. Lyssa looked at the centaur. 'I volunteer to fight Ladon, while you talk to the Hesperides. That way we increase our chances of winning.'

'If we're doing this, then I'm fighting too,' Lyssa said, but Evadne and Phyleus both shook their heads.

'No. If you want them to help, it will have to come from you,' Phyleus said.

She sighed and avoided looking at him, but he went on quietly. 'It's not something Hercules would think to try. And that alone makes it worth doing.'

IT WAS impossible not to realise you had reached Leo, as the entire realm was encased in dark, swirling clouds, filled with crackling purple lightning that sparked and rippled between gardens and arched doorways that were dotted amid the smog. Lyssa knew that if you entered any of those doorways you would be walking into one of the hundreds of floating mansions ringing the massive Mount Olympus that stood at Leo's centre. The view from the other side of those doors was breathtaking.

The *Alastor* flew until they found a pier jutting out high in the dense cloud, a concentration of the purple energy pulsing brighter than elsewhere. It was one of the ten gateways into Leo. As they reached it Lyssa gripped the railings hard, knowing what was coming next. The sparking energy would wrap around the ship, then suck them through. They visited Leo frequently, given that it was mostly the rich who required their services as smugglers. But as they drew alongside the pier there was a crack of thunder, so loud she winced, and the ship shot backwards fast. She reached out with her mind, slowing it down, and looked around for the source of the noise.

'Captain Lyssa,' cooed a voice from right behind her. She whirled around but there was nothing there.

Epizon, Nestor and Phyleus were running across the deck towards her.

'What's going on?' Phyleus panted, then yelped as a bird swooped over his head. Not just any bird, Lyssa saw, her breath catching. An eagle. Zeus famously took the form of an eagle.

'Zeus?' she called, tentatively.

There was a soft laugh and the bird banked and glided back, then angled towards the deck.

'No, no, dear child. I am Nereus.' The voice came from the air around them, but as the bird touched down there was a popping sound, and then an elderly, stooped man was standing on the deck of the *Alastor*.

'What are you doing on my ship?' Lyssa demanded, hand moving to the slingshot at her hip.

'Is that any way to greet an ally?' he said, his lips moving, the voice now clearly belonging to him.

'An ally?'

'Of course. I'm here to help. I can tell you where the Garden of the Hesperides is.'

'Why would you do that?' she asked suspiciously.

'I'm on strict orders from the gods, little one. I will be offering the same opportunity to the others. In fact, the *Hybris* is almost here, so I must hurry.'

'He's part of the Trial,' said Nestor, from behind her.

'Indeed I am. For today, at least. Tomorrow I may be a part of something else. Funny thing about shapeshifters,

you see: they can be part of anything they want to be.'
There was another pop, and Lyssa was staring into her
own eyes, messy red curls framing her surprised expression. She watched uneasily as her face on the
shapeshifter's body creased into laughter. 'I love my job, I
truly do,' Nereus said, then morphed back into an old
man. He was intensely unnerving, Lyssa decided.

'Where is the garden?' she asked him.

'It's not as easy as that, I'm afraid, child. I will leave
you with the information you need, but you will have to
decipher it. And you won't be able to copy your rivals.
They will be invisible to you until you have solved the
riddle. Are you listening?' She nodded. 'Very well.

Forests cover all of the northern islands of the realm
Fly low until you see the stone arches surrounded by elm
Five mighty arches bear a carved symbol of power
Four lead to monsters that would make you hide and
cower
One leads to an exquisite garden of bounty and beauty
Choose the path wisely: that shall be your heroic duty

'Good luck!' He smiled, then he was the eagle again,
leaping from the planks and soaring into the sky.

'Why is it always so bloody complicated!' Lyssa
seethed, stamping towards her crew.

'We'll work it out, Captain,' said Epizon.

7

HEDONE

'Well, at least we know we need to go to the northern islands,' Hedone said, frowning at the spot Nereus had just disappeared from.

'I knew that already,' Hercules snapped. 'Asterion, take us there quickly, we need to find these stone arches.'

'Yes, Captain,' the minotaur replied.

Hedone still wasn't sure how she felt about the massive beast she shared the ship with. It seemed odd to her that such a brutish creature could behave so submissively. He rarely spoke without being spoken to first, and he never offered his own opinion on anything. She wasn't even sure he had the capacity to form his own opinions.

'Why do they taunt us with puzzles and riddles? They prove nothing,' Hercules said, drawing Hedone's thoughts back to the riddle.

'I know, my love. But we are not fools; we will work it out. We need to figure out which of the arches is the right one. And they each bear a symbol of power...' She rubbed her cheek as she mused over Nereus's words. 'Maybe there will be more clues when we get there?' she said, hopefully. Hercules nodded, staring into the crackling clouds with his brows drawn together.

'We need to write it down, so that we have the words perfectly,' he said, and turned to her. 'Come on.' She reached for his outstretched hand and he led her to the hauler.

They made their way quickly to his chambers, where he began opening drawers in the chest by his huge book-shelves. He muttered and cursed as he moved things around and Hedone was sure she heard him say Evadne's name. If she remembered correctly, Evadne was good at puzzles. Like Theseus had been. A pang of painful guilt and regret hit her as Theseus's face floated before her, but it was gone before she could register what it meant.

'Here,' Hercules said, turning to her with a wad of paper and a pencil in his hands. 'Do you still remember it?'

'Yes,' she said and took them from him, resting the paper on her knees as she perched on the edge of the couch. Hercules moved behind her, watching over her shoulder as she wrote down, word for word, what Nereus had said, saying it aloud in the same sing-song tone the shapeshifter had used. The huge windows at the end of Hercules's bedroom, beyond the open doors, suddenly turned dark and her head snapped up to watch as dark clouds engulfed the ship. Hedone forced down the surge of panic as the light around them dimmed dramatically. They had reached the pier to enter Leo. Suddenly flashes of purple lit the smog, then there was a lurching sensa-tion and they shot forward. She almost lost her seating on the couch, but Hercules's strong arm wrapped around her shoulders in a heartbeat. And then they were through, bright blue sky filling the space beyond the glass again and causing her to let out a long breath of relief.

'Are you all right, my love?' Hercules asked her, his grip around her easing.

'Of course.' She swivelled around to face him, giving him a reassuring smile.

'Good. You'll get used to that, when we live here,' he said.

Her heart swelled, as it did every time he mentioned their future.

'I know I will. Thank you.'

He stared back into her eyes for a moment, his expression serious, then kissed her gently. Power and lust and heat flooded her body, and she kissed him back, letting the feelings wash over her. But he pulled away too quickly and she tried not to let her disappointment show her on face as he refocused on the paper on her lap.

'Now, it must be some sort of word puzzle, as there's no other clues here to a "symbol of power",' he said.

'Yes. You're right,' she answered, fixing her own attention as firmly as she could on the riddle.

8

LYSSA

Lyssa had no idea what the rhyme meant. At all. But Evadne, Phyleus, Len and Nestor were each adamant they could solve it first. It had almost turned into a competition, all four of them now spread across the deck, hunched over pieces of paper and chewing their lips. She was happy to leave them to it until they reached the islands. They were still about twenty minutes away and a bit of healthy competitiveness would probably improve their chances of solving it quickly.

Lyssa rested her arms on the railings of the quarter-deck and felt a wave of something akin to nostalgia as they sped over Mount Olympus. As usual, plenty of huge pleasure Zephyrs were making their way in a lazy circles around the beautiful mountain, and white stone mansions could be seen everywhere, floating amongst the crackling purple clouds. She avoided looking towards the one that belonged to Hercules. The one she had grown up in. She didn't miss the mansion, or Leo. But she missed her mother. She missed her little brother. She missed being part of a world where her worries were insignificant, and her dreams weren't haunted by blood and fury.

Perhaps she would have ended up with the same fears, the same nightmares, even if her past had played out differently, she told herself, as she watched Zeus's grand palace on the peak of the mountain get smaller as they zoomed onwards. Perhaps she would have ended up with a whole load of different problems, but nobody real to share them with. What would a life surrounded by Leo aristocracy have been like? That was exactly what Phyleus had run away from, she thought. He had told her that she was real, in a world of falseness. Sadness gripped her and she shut her eyes. She reached instinctively for the reassurance of her ship, and let the power seep into her. She was doing the right thing.

'Captain, we need to decide who is going to be involved in the Trial,' Epizon said from behind her.

'Yes,' she said, grateful for the interruption to her thoughts. 'How are you feeling? Do you want to fight? Or join me talking to the Hesperides?'

'As much as I would love to be with you, Captain, I fear I would be a hindrance if you needed to react quickly. I'm not strong enough to fight at my best.' His face was pinched and tight as he spoke and Lyssa knew what it cost him to say those words. He was truthful, sure, but he was also proud and fierce and no fighter wanted to admit they were weak.

'OK. Well, that's good, you can keep an eye on Evadne and Eryx. They're both staying on the ship.'

'Eryx is a good fighter, and fast. I think you should let

him go with Nestor and fight Ladon,' Epizon said, but she shook her head.

'No. Have you seen the look in his eyes when he's quiet? I know that look. As soon as he sees Hercules he'll lose it. And that will likely end up with him dead. He stays on the ship.'

'Then Nestor fights alone,' said Epizon. 'Phyleus must go with you.'

'Why must he?' She scowled.

'He brings out your emotions, which will add sincerity to your plea and make them more likely to want to help you. Plus he's more articulate than you,' he added with a small grin.

Lyssa stepped forward and punched him on the arm.

'I went to the academy in Leo, I'll have you know,' she said in her best posh voice.

'Could've fooled me,' Epizon shot back. She laughed.

'Yeah. I wasn't there long. Do you think Nestor will be all right, fighting alone?'

'Other than you and Eryx, she's the strongest on the ship. If anybody has a hope of getting past Ladon, it's her. And she will relish the opportunity.'

Lyssa nodded. She knew that much was true. And Hercules was less likely to make a target of the centaur than of someone he knew had been on Lyssa's crew a long time.

'OK. I'll tell her and Phyleus.'

9

EVADNE

E vadne stared hard at the riddle, her brain racing through possibilities as she processed the words. The uncomfortable planks she was sitting on and the hard railings she was leaning against faded to nothing as she focused on the challenge. This was exactly the chance she needed to prove herself to Lyssa. She was good at puzzles, really good. She needed to get the answer before the others. After spending so long feeling so useless and ignored on the *Hybris*, the desperation to excel now was almost overwhelming her. *Calm down*, she told herself, aware that her thoughts were racing too fast and fearful she would miss something. *Read it carefully*, she chided.

Forests cover all of the northern islands of the realm
Fly low until you see the stone arches surrounded by elm
Five mighty arches bear a carved symbol of power
Four lead to monsters that would make you hide and cower
One leads to an exquisite garden of bounty and beauty

Choose the path wisely: that shall be your heroic duty

It had to be a word puzzle, she was sure of that. There weren't enough clues for it to be anything else. *The first letter of each line makes...* She wrote the letters down, then scribbled them out. That didn't work. Far too many 'F's. The last letters? She wrote those down, then sighed and scribbled them out too. Was it an anagram? She began writing down words that stood out, rearranging the letters to try to form new words. She came up with nothing. There were six lines in the riddle, and the answer was a symbol of power. She probably needed one letter from each line to make up a word, she guessed. Maybe she could work backwards, see what would fit. The elements of power were well known in Olympus; Air, Earth, Fire, Water and Electricity. None of those words had six letters, though, she thought, biting the end of her pencil. Frowning, she tried to recall the books she'd read on ciphers and the puzzles she had played with as a child.

Six lines, one word. A thought struck her, and she began writing quickly. The first word from the first line, the second word from the second line, the third from the third. When she had written them down all she scanned the list and leaped to her feet, excitement thrilling through her.

'Captain? I've got it!' she called, trying to keep a huge smile off her face. Lyssa turned from the railings, where she was standing with Epizon, and raised her eyebrows.

'Really?'

'Really?' echoed Phyleus, getting up from where he'd been sitting against the mast.

'Yeah, really?' Len, the satyr, was trotting towards her, and Nestor strode up behind him.

'Yes, look.' She held out the paper, showing them all the list of words. 'First line, first word, second line, second word, et cetera,' she said, trying not to fidget as they leaned forward and inspected the paper.

Forests, Low, Arches, Monsters, Exquisite, Surely.

'Flames,' said Phyleus quietly, then beamed at her. 'The first letter of each word! Well done! I mean, I would have got there in the end, but that was quick.'

'Course, I would too, but yeah, well done,' added Len gruffly. Evadne let the smile spread across her face as Lyssa took the paper from her.

'Nice work. You're sure?' she asked, and Evadne could see the hesitance in her eyes as they flicked to Phyleus's.

'Yes. Positive,' she answered, knowing Lyssa really wanted to hear it from the others.

'It makes sense, Cap,' said Len. Lyssa nodded and turned back to Evadne.

'Good. If you're wrong, and I fly my longboat through this arch to a deadly monster and Hercules wins this Trial, the rest of my crew will make sure that you end up going through the wrong arch too. You got that?' she said, turning to Epizon.

'Got it. If you die, throw Evadne through the same arch to be killed by the monster,' Epizon said, standing up straight and nodding formally. Evadne looked at him wide-eyed until Lyssa strode towards the longboat and Epizon gave her an exaggerated wink. Eryx's grunts of protest behind her tailed off and she sagged in relief. She didn't doubt that the daughter of Hercules could be ruthless, not for a moment, but the more time she spent on the *Alastor*, the harder it was to believe that her big first mate would hurt a soul. She'd seen him fight, though, and she knew he was good. Guilt washed through her when she thought about Hercules nearly killing him on Scorpio. Thank the gods Epizon had survived.

'Captain, there's an island down there that looks like it has a big ring of trees on it,' called Abderos, his chair up against the railings on the quarterdeck. Lyssa jogged to the railings herself, leaning over.

'Lower the *Alastor*, see if we can spot any stone arches,' she said. Evadne felt the ship drop slightly, and moved to the railings too, peering down at a small island floating in the blue sky below them. She'd visited these islands as a child with her school, hiding from the other kids and their games up in the branches of the trees, where she'd get as comfortable as she could and read. 'I can see stone,' called Abderos. Evadne squinted until she could just make out the arches too.

'Right, Phyleus, Nestor: longboat now,' Lyssa barked, and then turned to Evadne, her face serious.

'Evadne, I'm trusting you because my crew seems to. On both the arch and talking to the Hesperides. Hercules will make many, many more lives miserable if he wins the Trials. This is your last chance to tell me if I'm making a mistake,' she said, her green eyes fierce.

'I want Hercules dead as much as you do,' Evadne said, holding her gaze. 'I swear, I'm telling you the truth. It's the fire arch, and you are more likely to get the apple from the Hesperides than by trying to defeat Ladon.' She projected her sincerity into the words, standing straight and holding her chin up.

'Good,' said Lyssa, after a beat. 'Then we'll see you soon.'

JUST MINUTES later Lyssa was in the boat with Phyleus and the centaur, the crew calling 'Good luck!' as they lifted off the deck of the *Alastor*.

'Nice work,' said Eryx, stepping up beside her as she watched the longboat zoom towards the arches below them.

'Thanks,' she said quietly. Her heart was racing. She believed she was right about the fire arch, but she wouldn't relax until she knew for sure.

'I think you're gaining her trust,' Eryx said, as the little boat swept past the arches.

'Hmm. Let's see if this works out before we get ahead of ourselves,' she muttered, and held her breath as the longboat paused before one arch, then sailed through, disappearing from sight.

10

LYSSA

L yssa took a deep breath as they passed through the arch that had flames carved all over its rough surface, only exhaling when they emerged into more clear blue sky. Ahead, a fair way below them, she could see a single tiny island. She didn't think it could be much bigger than a Zephyr ship. From above it looked like one massive, sprawling tree, with a ring of lush green grass around it.

Most of the islands on Leo had a magnetic pulling effect when you got close to the edge, and your feet would become so heavy you couldn't lift them at all, which meant you couldn't fall off. You could only move inland. She hoped this island was the same. It didn't look like it had a lot of room for fighting.

'I guess that's it,' she said, and the little boat sped towards the island. As the longboat moved lower Lyssa could see something moving amid the canopy, so slight that it looked like the branches themselves were alive.

This was the wrong colour for a branch, though. 'Is that Ladon?' she asked quietly.

'Where?' replied Phyleus, squinting and leaning over the side of the boat.

'Moving amongst the branches,' said Nestor, her gaze steady and fierce. 'Yes, I believe it is.'

'Where are the Hesperides? This plan is useless if we have to get past Ladon to reach them.'

'I guess we'll have to land and find out.' Phyleus shrugged.

Lyssa lowered the longboat onto the lip of grass around the tree, keeping as close to the edge as she dared. Nestor leaped from the boat as soon as they touched down.

Phyleus followed her, then held his hand out to Lyssa. Just a few weeks ago she would have scoffed, told him she didn't need his help climbing out of a longboat, but the sadness in his warm eyes made her press her lips tight together. She took his hand, and jumped down onto the soft grass.

'Captain Lyssa,' a deep, silky voice hissed. She whirled around, looking up at the tree. It was, without a doubt, the most stunning example of any tree she'd ever seen.

It was nothing like the mighty giants that stretched to the sky on Taurus, or the broad leafy trees making up the humid forests on Cancer and Gemini. Instead, it was unnaturally symmetrical, the solid trunk hosting ever-widening branches that curved up and around into a dense ball of wood and greenery. Veins of gold glittered through the bark, almost like they were liquid, rolling and shimmering in streams and running into the deep green leaves, rippling out in complicated patterns. Lyssa could easily believe that this tree would bear fruit made of solid gold. It oozed power and beauty and luxury.

A deep burgundy colour caught her eye amongst the glittering gold and bright green. It was everywhere, she realised as she concentrated, slithering in and out of the branches.

'Ladon?' she called aloud. She had expected an unevolved creature when Zeus had described Ladon as his pet. Surely he wouldn't keep an intelligent dragon trapped on a tiny island like this? There were so few left in Olympus.

'I welcome your visit,' the voice replied. 'We get lonely, here alone.'

'We?'

'Yes. The Hesperides and I.'

'How long have you been here?' she asked.

'Lyssa, who are you talking to?' hissed Phyleus.

'You can't hear him?' She turned to Phyleus in surprise.

'Hear who?' The dragon chuckled and the sound sent shivers through her body.

'I am only talking to you, Captain Lyssa. Although that young man is interesting indeed. He has the ichor of Hades in his veins.'

'How do you know that?' Lyssa stared up at the tree, trying to discern some distinct features of the dragon, but all she could see were flashes of deep red.

'I am ancient. More ancient than you can imagine. And I don't see or feel in a way that you could comprehend. For instance, I know that you have extremely precious cargo on your ship.'

Lyssa bit her lip, frustration and a frisson of fear muddying her thoughts, but sending pulses of power through her muscles as well. If Ladon knew Tenebrae was on the ship, then Zeus would soon too.

'We're here for an apple. May we have one?' she called back, ignoring his comment. The dragon laughed again.

'Absolutely not. I must guard these with my life. You know, one of these apples caused a war once.'

Lyssa clenched her fists as Nestor stepped forward.

'Ladon?' the centaur called.

'Hello, little centaur, tool of Artemis.' The dragon's voice rang out loudly, and Lyssa almost jumped in surprise.

'I am no more a tool of a god than you are, Ladon,' she answered. 'Zeus told us we could kill you, for an apple. Does that not anger you?'

'If I am killed, I will be reborn. Although I doubt very much you would be able to end my life. Nobody has managed that in thousands of years.'

Lyssa could hear the smile in the dragon's voice. Adrenaline was starting to surge around her body, making her impatient and angry.

'Show yourself!' she shouted.

'Lyssa!' Phyleus hissed beside her. 'We're not supposed to be—' But his words were cut off by a ripping, slithering sound. The tree creaked as an enormous, exquisite dragon emerged from the foliage.

Lyssa had seen pictures of dragons, and seen them in flame dishes, but Ladon in the flesh was utterly breath-taking. His body was mostly snakelike, but he had short legs ending in clawed feet, which were gripping the tree trunk as he slithered down towards them. His head was ringed by an orange-and-gold mane that moved like fire, and flames danced in his intelligent, inky black eyes. The skin on his delicately scaled face shimmered, and vicious teeth lined his long snout. Two long wispy whiskers projected from above his flaring nostrils, probing the air ahead of him as he came to a stop halfway down the trunk. His head was the size of the longboat, at least.

Power hammered through Lyssa's body, all of her instincts preparing her to fight. She *wanted* to fight. The challenge in Ladon's eyes sang to her, calling her forward. Had she ever faced a creature so impressive?

'Lyssa,' Phyleus said, and she realised the voice was in her head. 'Lyssa, this is not the plan.'

'New plan,' she answered curtly, as Ladon took another slow step down the tree trunk. There was a metallic sound as Nestor drew her warhammer from its sling on her belt.

'No, Lyssa. Hercules will be here soon. We must find the Hesperides. You can't...' He trailed off and she looked at him.

'You think I can't beat him?' she said aloud, and the dragon's laugh made the Rage pulse harder within her.

'Of course he thinks you can't beat me! He's less stupid

than you are,' Ladon boomed, the flames leaping to life in his irises. Lyssa bared her teeth, dropping her weight, preparing herself. She had Zeus's own power within her. She could beat Ladon. She could beat anybody.

'And here your mighty father is now,' sang Ladon, his voice silky again.

11

HEDONE

'Hercules, please, I could help!' Hedone pleaded, as Hercules climbed into the longboat after Asterion.

'No! I will just worry that you will be in harm's way. We've discussed this!'

Frustration welled up in Hedone.

'But I'm fast, and I'll stay away from the dragon. I can't bear the thought of being so far from you and so useless, you must understand that?' She poured her power into her words, making them as seductive as she possibly could. Hercules's severe expression softened.

'My love, I equally couldn't bear it if you were in danger.'

'Then you will fight even harder. Perhaps that's what Zeus meant about you needing others. It's not because you are not enough on your own, but because you need a stronger motivation.'

He stared at her for a few heartbeats, considering.

'You are as wise as you are beautiful,' he said eventually. 'Get in.' She suppressed her squeal of triumph, and took his hand, climbing into the small boat. 'Stay well away from the tree. You shouldn't be able to fall off the island if it's like the others in Leo. Don't do anything that might endanger your life.'

'Yes.' She nodded. 'Of course. I'll do exactly as you tell me.'

The longboat lifted from the deck of the *Hybris* and her hair fluttered around her face. She would help Hercules at any cost.

HEDONE COULDN'T HELP the gasp that escaped her lips as they landed on the small island.

The dragon was huge, and absolutely stunning. The white centaur, Lyssa and Phyleus were standing opposite him, Lyssa tense and crouching slightly, clearly ready to fight. The centaur was holding a gleaming hammer aloft.

'Stay here,' Hercules said to Hedone, as all eyes turned to them.

'How will you kill it?' she breathed in awe as Hercules pulled *Keravnos* from its sheath.

'Just watch,' he said, and stepped from the boat.

'HERCULES, WELCOME!' The dragon said, and Hedone's mouth fell open. 'We were just discussing your arrival.' The creature's deep, lyrical voice gave a sense of great age. Hedone stared at his massive teeth as his jaw moved. For all his impressive beauty, there was no doubt Ladon was still a monster. Fear for Hercules thrummed through her as he strode forward.

'I'm glad to be here,' he called. 'My daughter and I have unfinished business, as it happens.' He turned to Lyssa but before he could speak again the girl spat at him.

'Don't fucking call me that!' she yelled and Hedone was sure she going to spring at him.

'I fear I'm no longer the centre of your attention,' the dragon said loudly, and they both turned back to him. He was slowly making his way to the ground, his body slithering against the tree bark, which was pulsing with gold rivulets. 'You have both come for a golden apple. Your half-giant rival will arrive in a while,' he said, and his eyes flicked to Lyssa. 'I'm sure you wouldn't want to lose your hard-won advantage,' he said, his eyes flicking to Lyssa. His point was clear. She'd wasted her head start and now had to compete with Hercules.

'I agree,' said Hercules, turning his face to Lyssa, eyes narrowed. 'I don't want to kill you now, girl. You will watch as I defeat this dragon and become immortal. And then you will spend the rest of your short, insignificant life losing everyone you love one by one, at my hand.'

Keravnos glowed as he raised the sword above his head, and charged at Ladon.

12

LYSSA

'Lyssa, for the sake of the gods, will you listen to me!' Phyleus's voice thundered through Lyssa's raging thoughts and she spun to face him as Hercules hurled himself towards the dragon. 'Leave him to be torn apart by Ladon! We're not here for revenge right now, we're here to get that apple!'

The sense in his words penetrated the fog of Rage and she let out a snarl.

'I want to kill him, Phyleus! I can't... I can hardly control my power around him now,' she said, gritting her teeth. She heard a thud and turned to see *Keravnos* being buried into the trunk of the stunning tree, then Ladon's tail flicking out of nowhere and sending Hercules flying backwards, swordless. Nestor roared on her other side, and began to canter towards the dragon.

'Then we get away from him. Come on, I've got an idea,' Phyleus said, and grabbed her hand, tugging her away from the tree. Lyssa resisted for a second, her body refusing to leave the impending battle, but he tugged harder, and her feet began to move. He pulled her to the longboat, and Lyssa shot one last reluctant look at Nestor as the centaur launched her hammer at the dragon's head and swerved away from its snapping jaws, before she willed the boat into the air.

'Where are we going?' she asked him as they rose.

'Underneath the island.'

'What?'

'There's nothing else up here, and nowhere else to look!'

THEY SOARED AWAY from the island, then as soon as they cleared the edge they dove, the little boat dropping through the clear sky. Lyssa held her breath as they took in the underside of the island, then let it out slowly. There was nothing there but shallow, bare rock.

Phyleus groaned beside her. Lyssa's hands curled into fists again and she pressed her lips firmly together to stop the torrent of swearing escaping. 'Fly underneath,' Phyleus said and she glared at him. 'We're here now, we may as well check it properly!' he protested.

'Fine,' she barked, and guided the longboat under the island.

A blast of warmth engulfed them, and suddenly the longboat began to spin.

'Lyssa!' Phyleus yelled, and she reached for him as she tumbled from where she was crouched in the boat. He threw both his arms around her and they fell hard together. The spinning didn't stop or even slow down and they were thrown around the hull of the little boat, disorientation making her feel sick. Then there was a jolt and a crash and they weren't moving any more.

13

ERYX

Eryx watched in the flame dish as Hercules rolled out of Ladon's reach and swiped his sword up from where he had dropped it on the ground. He was grinding his teeth so hard it hurt.

'How is this helping?' he shouted suddenly, and Abderos and Evadne jumped. 'I should be down there!' He leaped to his feet and stamped away from the dish, anger making his movements heavy. He leaned against the railings of the *Alastor*, looking down at the tree on the island far below. How was he supposed to avenge his captain's death and help Lyssa from up here? She was a fool for leaving him here, impotent.

'You'll get your chance,' Evadne said from behind him. He didn't turn around.

'This *was* my chance. I'm a fighter, it's what I do. It's *all* I can do, and I'm stuck here, watching others fight.' He banged his fist against the rickety rail. 'I hate this,' he said, bitterly.

'I'd say let's steal a longboat and go help, but there's

no way down there,' she said, apologetically. He sighed, and turned to look at her.

'Well, thanks for the thought,' he muttered. A sudden, blinding flash of white light made him shield his eyes and he heard Evadne shout in surprise. His heart was racing as he lowered his arm, and he inhaled sharply as he dropped to his knees.

'Poseidon,' he breathed, not daring to lift his head and look at the god. *Poseidon was here*. His father, just a few feet front of him. Eryx realised he was breathing too shallowly, and tried to slow his galloping heart.

'Rise.' The god's voice rang out. 'I do not have long here.' Eryx stumbled to his feet. 'I am sorry about Antaeus. He was a good man. You will have to assume his quest now,' Poseidon said. Eryx was sure he could see actual waves, white and blue and crashing, in the god's eyes.

'His quest?'

'My brother Zeus's hero is a cruel moron,' said Poseidon, his lip curling as he spoke. 'I have no desire to see Hercules immortal. In the second Trial you won a key from the Hydra. You will need that key, Eryx.' He turned to Evadne, and the girl's face instantly flushed scarlet. 'You will be able to work out what to do with it.' She gaped at him, her jaw moving but no words forming. Poseidon rolled his eyes and turned back to Eryx. 'The *Orion* will be here soon. Get on the ship and retrieve that key.'

'How will we get there?' Eryx stammered. Poseidon frowned for a moment, then flicked his wrist. A longboat appeared on the quarterdeck behind them, and Eryx blinked at it. The sides of the boat were not plain, but carved in pale blue waves, and the small sail was a shining teal colour. 'You may keep this longboat,' Poseidon said, after a second's silence. 'I believe you deserve it,' he said, then vanished.

14

HERCULES

Hercules rolled again, awkwardly angling *Keravnos* so that he didn't slash himself with his own sword. Gods, Ladon was fast! Whenever Hercules tried to get above him he would slither back into the tree, then reappear a heartbeat later, ahead. The dragon was also successfully fending off Asterion and the centaur from Lyssa's crew, and laughing while he did it. Anger strengthened Hercules's muscles and he powered out of reach of a swiping claw.

'Ladon! You're my father's pet! Shouldn't you be helping me?' he shouted, as a tail whipped towards him from the branches. He jumped over it, and ran towards the tree trunk. The dragon's laugh boomed in his mind.

'Poor little Hercules, always caught in the middle of your father's mistakes. Zeus keeps me here, whether I want to be or not. I owe his kin nothing.'

'He will punish you for saying such a thing,' Hercules panted.

'The lord of the gods has some limits, you know. None

of the Olympians can read minds. Only an oracle has that gift.'

Asterion ran up to Hercules, breathing hard.

'He's too fast, Captain.'

Hercules glanced up, spotting a golden apple glinting high above him in the foliage.

'Climb,' he growled to Asterion. The minotaur frowned at him.

'But, Captain, I can't climb.' He looked down at his hooved feet.

'Then use your arms!' Hercules bellowed, then shoved him aside as Ladon's head dipped out of the tree to their right, huge teeth gnashing at them. He swung *Keravnos* and almost caught the end of the one the creatures' probing whiskers. The dragon withdrew with a snort. 'You're just a pet, Ladon. A toy belonging to a god. You're hardly ancient or mighty.'

'You can't beat me, little man,' the dragon boomed. 'I don't think I like you.' Hercules started to run again, towards where he had seen a flash of red in the lower branches.

'Stop wrapping yourself around this blasted tree and fight in the open like a real opponent!' he roared.

'You want me to leave the tree?'

With unnatural speed, Ladon erupted from the branches, his massive body writhing effortlessly above his short legs. He had jumped clear overhead and as Hercules whirled around, sword raised, his heart almost stopped. The dragon was speeding towards Hedone.

15

HEDONE

By the time Hedone realised the dragon was aiming for her, it was too late. She tried to duck down into the longboat but Ladon was too fast. She screamed as his clawed hand closed around her waist and she was lifted off her feet. The dragon didn't stop moving and the air was knocked from her lungs by the impact, cutting off her shriek and making her gasp as the world around her flew by in a green blur.

'Sorry, lovely little goddess.' His voice slithered through her mind. 'But I need to teach that captain of yours a lesson.' He had taken her into the tree, Hedone realised, struggling in Ladon's grip to look around her. Gold-veined leaves surrounded them, soft against her skin as they kept moving. Fear pulsed through her, and she thrashed hard.

'Put me down!' she commanded mentally, as fiercely as she could manage. Her hair was bouncing around her face and she could hardly see as Ladon chuckled. She beat her hands uselessly against his massive black claws.

'Are you going to kill me?' she asked, throwing her arms protectively over her head as they crashed through branches.

'You're far too lovely to kill,' he answered after a pause. Hedone hoped he was telling the truth.

'He'll get an apple while you're up here playing with me,' she shot at him.

'Dear girl, my head and tail are still below the tree, toying with these fools. I have been guarding this fruit a very, very long time.'

'Well, he has more than just the apples to fight for now!' she said, the irony of her words striking her. That was why she had wanted to come, to spur him on. She bit her lip as she came to a stop, deep amid the foliage.

'Tell me, how can a thing as delicate as you be in love with a brute like him?' Ladon mused in her head. Hedone pushed her hair away from her face, scanning the branches around her. Ladon's massive fist had protected her body from being scratched, but her arms were covered in shallow scrapes and her hair was full of leaves and twigs.

'He's not what everybody thinks he is,' she answered, trying uselessly to pull at the claws around her.

'He's exactly what everyone thinks he is. I sense a power over you that is not your own.' Hedone stilled, her face creasing into a frown. 'The power of an Olympian. Tell me, child, have you felt confused recently? Unable to gather your thoughts?' Hedone's heart pounded and shivers ran over her skin. *Yes*. She recalled all those moments where something important had seemed just out of her reach. But then the image of

Hercules's face replaced them, large and handsome and fierce.

'So what if I have? Theseus lied to me and led me on for years; of course I would be confused when I found a man who truly loved me.' Ladon laughed, long and loud, and anger washed over her. 'Put me down!' she screamed, beating at his claws again with renewed vigour.

'The gods are cruel, little goddess. I do not envy you your future.'

'My future will be with Hercules!' Hedone shouted, tears filling her eyes. Why was he putting her through this, making her doubt her own feelings? 'When this is over we will be together, and the gods will finally leave him alone! He will heal.'

A sob escaped her. The dragon said nothing.

16

LYSSA

'Are you OK?' Phyleus asked, trying to sit. Lyssa was sprawled across him, and she pushed herself up fast, shoving her hair out of her face.

'Yeah, are you?'

'Yeah. What...' He trailed off as they both stood, taking in where they were. 'The Garden of the Hesperides,' he breathed. And it was one hell of a garden. There were flowers everywhere. The smell of them should have been overpowering, but Lyssa inhaled deeply, the scent calming her. Ahead of them was a long pool that seemed to stretch across the whole island, and bridges with ornate, curling railings connected little islands of bright flower beds, delicate trees or swinging cushioned seats. At intervals there were fountains around the banks, statues of all sorts of creatures pouring glittering water from jugs and urns. Either side of the pool there were bushes and hedges that had been clipped into the shapes of even more creatures, pristine and neat and surrounded by white daisies.

'Hello,' breathed a voice, and one of the nearby trees shimmered and morphed into a stunning young woman. Phyleus coughed loudly, and stumbled in the boat. The woman was naked, save for a ring of interlocked baby-blue flowers hanging around her neck. Her long blonde hair fell to her waist and she cocked her head as she smiled at them. Lyssa felt her own face heat a little.

'Hi,' she said, awkwardly.

'We don't have visitors here very often,' came another lilting voice, and all around them, plants and fine trees morphed into more beautiful naked women, wearing different coloured flowers around their necks. Lyssa looked at Phyleus, who had fixed his eyes on the face of the first woman who had spoken and appeared to be doing his best to keep them there. She rolled her eyes, trying to squash the instinct to compare her own body unfavourably with these girls.

'We don't mean to disturb you,' she said, stepping out of the boat. The grass was bouncy under her feet and a wave of that delicious, fresh floral smell wafted over her.

'Not at all. It is a pleasure to have company,' another woman said, a huge smile on her full lips. 'Would you like a drink? Some fruit?'

'Err, as it happens, some fruit is exactly what we would like,' said Phyleus.

'Of course,' a red-haired woman said, and she held out her hands. Fruits of all different sizes and colours, most of which Lyssa didn't recognise, appeared from nowhere, filling her arms.

'Actually, we have been sent by Zeus to get a golden apple,' she said.

The women all froze, then turned to her as one.

'Zeus knows you're here?' the first woman said, quietly.

'Yes. We are competing in a Trial he set us, to gain immortality,' Phyleus said.

'We are immortal. It is not as desirable as you might think,' a woman with short black hair said.

Lyssa frowned at her.

'Are you goddesses?'

'No. We are wood nymphs, of a sort. We were created by Zeus, for Zeus.'

'He visits with us, but he does not love us,' another nymph added.

'Oh. I'm sorry,' Lyssa answered her, unsure if it was the right thing to say. 'Well, we are competing against a man who is very cruel. And we are less interested in immortality than we are in keeping him from it.'

'Is that who is fighting with precious Ladon now?' asked a blonde nymph with wide eyes. Lyssa nodded.

'He is strong,' said another. Lyssa's eye twitched as she looked at her.

'Yes. And he is a murderer.'

'That matters not to us. We are so terribly lonely.' The first nymph stepped forward and the rest followed her, closing in around them. Unease slid over Lyssa, her senses alert and her body tensing.

'I'm sorry you're lonely. Are you able to help us?' she asked, levelly.

'We are able, yes. But we are not willing.'

Lyssa took a step backwards, reaching behind her to feel for the longboat.

'Why not?' asked Phyleus, as the nymphs closed in further.

'You haven't offered us anything in return.'

'Oh. What would you like? We have money, back on our ship,' he said.

The nymphs laughed as one, the sound tinkling and gentle and lovely.

'What would we do with money? No, no. We desire company.' Every one of the nymphs' beautiful faces fixed on Phyleus, and their predatory gazes made Lyssa's blood ran cold.

'Ohhh no. I don't know what you're thinking, but we are leaving,' she said, reaching for Phyleus's arm. 'Thanks for your time,' she said quickly, pulling him towards her.

'Wait,' he said, turning to face her. 'Let's hear them out.'

She raised her eyebrows.

'No!'

He tugged his arm out of her grip.

'Yes,' he said, and turned back to the blonde nymph. 'What would you like in return for a golden apple?'

'You,' she said.

'Time to go,' Lyssa barked, grabbing his arm again, but he stepped out of her reach.

'Lyssa, wait. Think about it.'

'I don't need to. Let's go.'

'You said yourself, if Hercules wins the Trials then he will hunt you forever.' His eyes softened as they bored into hers. 'Lyssa, I wasn't supposed to survive the Elysium Mysteries. I was given a second chance, and maybe this was why. For a higher cause.'

Lyssa stared at him, her brain refusing to process what he was saying.

'You want to stay here?' she whispered, her heart racing.

'Of course not. But if it gives you a life free of him... I would do anything for that.'

Tears filled Lyssa's eyes as emotion engulfed her, everything she had crushed down and refused to feel spilling over at once. He was willing to give up his own life for her to be free. And in that moment, Lyssa realised it was too late. It was too late to push him out, to save herself the pain of losing someone she loved. Because if she lost him, right then, she knew wouldn't be able to carry on. She already loved him.

'I need you,' she whispered, staring at his set, beautiful face. 'I don't want to be free without you.' His lips parted and the look in his eyes changed, hope replacing the sadness. 'Phyleus, I'd rather run for a lifetime with you by my side than spend a single minute free of him without you,' she said, the truth of the words sending bolts of power and joy through her body as she spoke them. 'I love you.'

His hands were on her face in a second, and he wiped a tear away with his thumb as he tilted her face up and whispered,

'Say that again.'

'I love you.'

He kissed her, and it was so much more than it had been before. Passion gave way to an emotion so tangible she felt like she would explode as it shuddered through her body. His hands were in her hair now, and she brought her own fingers to his face, feeling his skin, pulling him even closer. She would never, ever let him go, Hercules and immortality be damned.

17

EVADNE

E vadne cast a last, nervous glance over her shoulder as the wave-carved longboat lifted silently from the deck of the *Alastor*. Epizon gave them a silent wave and she lifted her hand in response. Abderos had seen Poseidon with his own eyes, so there was no way any of the crew of the *Alastor* were going to object to their little mission.

Why did Poseidon want Eryx to have the Hydra key, she wondered, curiosity burning inside her. Evadne hadn't known that Athena had shown interest in Eryx way back in the second Trial until he'd told her. She felt a sliver of hope and tried to push it back down. She had made peace with her decision. She was happy to give up her shot at immortality; that wasn't why she was still fighting in the Trials. She was there for Eryx now. Watching his face as Poseidon's praise sank in was genuinely one of the best moments of her life, and the strength of her happiness for him cemented what she had come to realise last night in the cargo deck. The simple, honest and loyal man was the only thing she really cared about any more.

'Busiris will not try to fight Ladon. I fear he will still be on the *Orion*,' Eryx said, as the little boat sped towards the Zephyr, which was hovering by the small island.

'Will you fight him? Or should we try to be stealthy?' she asked.

He turned to look at her.

'What do you think we should do?'

Hercules had never once asked her that question and her heart filled with a surge of happiness.

'The easiest way is stealth. But I know you're angry with him, and I understand if you want to challenge him.' She paused and cocked her head. 'Do you want to try to take back the *Orion*?'

Eryx's eyebrows shot up, and Evadne realised he hadn't even considered the idea. How different he was to most fighters.

'Take the *Orion*? I wouldn't know where to start. I'd have no crew, and...' Pain settled over his broad face. 'No,' he said, shaking his head. 'Antaeus was a captain. He didn't make me his first mate because he knew I would not be good at it. We stick to the plan and help Captain Lyssa defeat Hercules,' he stated, resolutely. Evadne nodded.

'OK. But just so you know, I think you'd make a great captain.' She gave him her warmest smile and his piercing blue eyes lit up.

'Really?'

'Sure. With me to help, of course.' She grinned.

'You would stay with me?'

'Eryx, I think you may be stuck with me for some time.'

'I'm glad about that,' he said quietly.

'Me too,' she said, and leaned forward and kissed him on the cheek. His skin flushed instantly and she couldn't help the giggle that escaped her lips.

'I've never met anybody like you,' she said as he glared at her indignantly.

'Hmmm,' he grunted.

'I meant that as a compliment.'

'Oh. Well, then... I've never met anybody like you either.'

THE LONGBOAT SILENTLY APPROACHED THE *Orion*, staying well below the deck, so they would run less risk of being seen. They knew from experience that Evadne could climb through the portholes in the living quarters, or through the ballista windows. However, they couldn't see any open portholes as they sailed around the huge hull of the ship, so they headed lower, to the weapons deck.

'Are you sure about this?' hissed Eryx, as Evadne leaned over the side of the little boat and gripped the wooden frame of the ballista window.

'Yes, of course,' she whispered, looking back over her shoulder at his worried face. 'If Busiris is on board, he'll never even know I was there. I'll be in and out before you miss me.' She gave him a small smile, and pulled herself through the window, squeezing past the huge weapon and landing lightly on the planks on the other side. She wasted no time, jogging as quickly and quietly as she could to the corridor, and scanning for the hauler. Though the ship was big, she had her bearings enough to know roughly where Eryx's room was, and he had told her which drawer in his chest contained the Hydra key.

The hauler doors slid open as soon as she tugged on them, and she stepped inside, nervous energy skittering through her. When she reached the living quarters deck, she pulled the hauler doors open again, and ran down the corridor to the left. The Zephyr felt so different to the *Hybris*, the wood lacking that deep mahogany shine, the planks that made up the ceiling above her head so much higher. She ran past massive doors on both sides, trying to keep count. She was almost certain that Eryx's room was the fourth from the end, on her left. She heard a loud clatter, and slowed down, her heart leaping hard in her chest. So Busiris *was* on board.

Was that a noise from the galley? She turned her head to look behind her, trying to work out which way the sound had come from. Lots of galleys didn't have doors, so if she ran past she might be spotted. She slowed almost to a stop, listening intently for a clue to Busiris's location.

'Well, well, well.' A rasping, snide voice made her jump, her blood suddenly turning cold in her veins. She whirled around to see Busiris step fully into the corridor just a few feet ahead of her. 'Come to take the ship back, have you?'

His black eyes were narrowed, and he was holding a kitchen knife. An image of Hercules holding a similar knife in the galley of the *Hybris* flashed before her, and her knees felt suddenly weak.

'Well, you can't have it! The *Orion* is mine!' Busiris yelled, and lunged forward.

Evadne moved as fast as her legs would carry her, sprinting back down the corridor the way she had come, the half-giant's footsteps pounding behind her. She felt his grip on her shoulder too soon, his long legs easily outpacing hers, and she kicked out as he spun her to face him. There was fury in his expression, the cold, calm front he usually wore nowhere to be seen. He gripped her shoulder harder as he towered over her, holding the knife in front of her face. She stilled, breathing hard, shaking.

'Let's see if Eryx wants to join us, shall we?' Busiris hissed.

Egypt was ruled by Busiris, a son of Poseidon. He sacrificed all strangers on an alter to Zeus, after a seer told him that killing a stranger would end famine. Busiris sacrificed the seer first, then slaughtered all strangers who came to Egypt.

EXCERPT FROM

THE LIBRARY BY APOLLODORUS

Written 300–100 BC

Paraphrased by Eliza Raine

18

ERYX

'E RYX!'

He was so startled to hear his name bellowed from overhead that his whole body jumped, his heart leaping with it. Concern for Evadne filled his brain before any other thoughts could take hold.

'Eryx, come and face me!'

His fists clenched as Busiris's voice carried across the still blue sky. He urged the longboat up, towards the deck of the Zephyr, and cold anger gripped him as he crested the railings. Busiris was standing in the centre of the deck, his gold skin shining. Evadne was tied to the middle mast, a gag wrapped around her mouth.

'Ah! So good of you to join us! And here I was thinking about how you can possibly have the nerve to call me a coward. You sent a girl to do your job? Were you too scared to face me, brother?'

'You're no brother to me,' Eryx spat, as Poseidon's longboat sank to the deck. 'Let her go, now.' Busiris took a step backwards, towards Evadne, and raised his hand, showing Eryx the knife he held.

'I told you not to trust her, but you wouldn't listen. Now it seems you may have been right. Who'd have thought it, eh? The simple, stupid Eryx got something right.' Busiris sneered, then turned back to Evadne. Her eyes were cold and hard, her jagged hair falling around her face. 'She can tell me what I need to know to get to Hercules. There's still a chance I can win this.'

Eryx snorted and stepped towards them. He could hear the pounding of his own heart in his ears, restless energy making it hard to keep his movements slow and measured. He forced himself to keep his eyes on Busiris instead of Evadne.

'You still think you can win this? You're mad. You lost any chance of winning when you left Antaeus to die.'

This time Busiris snorted.

'Hercules was going to kill him, no matter what I did.'

'You're a coward.' Eryx took another step forward.

'You call it cowardice, I call it sense,' Busiris hissed, baring his teeth. 'Only a fool runs towards his own death.'

'Only a coward believes that they cannot stop their own death.'

Busiris barked out a laugh. 'You think either of us could survive Hercules, son of Zeus, strongest mortal in Olympus? You're an idiot, Eryx.'

'Together, we could have stopped him!' Eryx shouted, his calm slipping. 'With Antaeus, fighting together, we could have stopped what happened!'

Busiris glared at him a moment, then turned back to Evadne.

'Let's ask your new girlfriend what she thinks.' He ripped the gag from her mouth. 'Well? You should know better than anyone: do you think little Eryx here could have beaten your old boyfriend?'

Eryx tried not to flinch at the words.

'Go to hell,' Evadne spat. Busiris laughed.

'I'll take that as a no, then. But since we're talking, how do I get onto the *Hybris*? There must be a weakness on the ship somewhere.'

'Eryx is right, you've gone mad. You can't win this,' she said, struggling inside the ropes. Eryx took another step closer. 'What good would breaking into the *Hybris* do you? Hercules would just kill you as soon as he found you. You're nothing to him.'

Busiris's onyx eyes flashed.

'You know... you're right,' he said, a slow smile spreading across his face. 'You've just given me a brilliant idea! I need to win him over. Trade my way onto his crew. And as it happens, I have just the bargaining chip. I do believe he would pay handsomely for a chance to get even with the girl who shot him in front of the world.'

Fear filled Evadne's eyes and Eryx's fragile control snapped. He roared as he threw himself at Busiris, bringing his arm down hard on the wrist that held the knife. It clattered to the deck, spinning away as the two half-giants stumbled backwards towards the rear mast. Eryx had never once sparred with Busiris, and he was surprised his charge hadn't toppled the gold man. He was stronger than Eryx had given him credit for.

Busiris shoved back at him as he regained his footing,

locking his arms around Eryx's. He tried to pull away, but the gold man's grip on his shoulders was too tight.

'There's a reason you've never seen me fight, little Eryx,' Busiris hissed, his face just inches from Eryx's own. 'You think I became a king by being weak? You think Antaeus didn't know what I was made of?'

'You were on this crew because you had money, not because you had his respect,' Eryx snarled.

'Is that what he told you? He was only captain of this ship because his brute strength made him impossible to challenge, and he knew one day I would take his place. All I had to do was wait for my chance,' Busiris said, a nasty smile on his lips. Anger swelled inside Eryx. 'Antaeus wasn't as stupid as you,' Busiris sneered. 'Antaeus feared me.'

'You're a lying, cowardly snake!' Eryx yelled, then ducked, yanking down hard enough to break Busiris's lock on his arms. He darted to his left, then braced his shoulder and smashed sideways into Busiris's ribs as hard as he possibly could. He heard the air leave the half-giant's lungs as he flew across the deck, and his own momentum carried him forward a few staggering paces. There was a thud as Busiris hit the planks, then continued to skid towards the railings. A loud crack was followed by a yell, then the gold half-giant was flailing, waving his arms wildly, and Eryx raced forward as he realised what was happening. Busiris's weight had broken the railings.

'Help me!' he gasped, his legs disappearing over the edge of the ship, broken bits of wooden rail dropping past him. Indecision tore at Eryx as his pace slowed. Busiris didn't deserve to live, but going overboard, all the way up here? Eryx didn't even know when the fall would stop; there was nothing below Leo. And was it really his place to choose to end the man's life?

The fear filling Busiris's eyes as his chest began to slip below the edge of the *Orion*'s deck, his fingers scrabbling madly on the smooth planks, made Eryx's mind up for him. He reached out his arm as he dropped to a crouch, inches from closing his fist around Busiris's hand when the half-giant's black eyes widened suddenly, and with a shout he was gone.

Eryx lunged forward, gripping the edge of the deck tightly, and instantly regretted it when he saw the terror on Busiris's face as he plummeted into nothingness.

19

LYSSA

Lyssa never wanted the kiss to end. At that moment, in that place where only she and Phyleus existed, the Trials meant nothing. All that mattered was that they were together. When Phyleus pulled away from her, short of breath, his face as flushed as she knew her own to be, she blinked at him. Why had he stopped?

'We'll fight Ladon, and we'll just have to win,' he said quietly. Her senses trickled back in through the passion, the stakes they were fighting for reasserting themselves. They weren't just fighting for their own freedom, they were trying to stop Hercules from having an endless lifetime to hurt others. They would have time to be together, as soon as this was over.

'Maybe Nestor is already doing well,' she said and nodded, reluctant to step further back from him, to take her hands from his chest and the back of his neck.

'She is not.' The nymph's voice was like ice water dousing her hot skin, and she dragged her hands from Phyleus as he turned back to face the beautiful blonde.

'Then we must go and help her. Thank you for your time,' he said politely, inclining his head. Lyssa scowled, refusing to follow suit.

'Wait. What you two have found is more than any of us could dream of,' the nymph said, her voice soft. Lyssa narrowed her eyes and gripped Phyleus's hand in her own.

'We are privileged to see the power of real love,' said another nymph, and Lyssa was surprised to see tears rolling down the young girl's face.

'To sacrifice yourself for another is truly heroic. This man you seek to stop, he would put an end to your love?'

'Yes. He has promised to kill her,' Phyleus said, gesturing at Lyssa. Muttering rippled through the crowd of nymphs, their pretty faces creasing into frowns.

'Very well. You may take this, on the condition that you nurture your love above all else. It is precious and you must never forget that few are so lucky.'

Lyssa's breath caught as the nymph's hands began to glow, brighter and brighter gold. When the light faded, a single, gleaming golden apple lay cupped in her palms.

Phyleus stepped forward, and Lyssa went after him, refusing to let go of his hand.

'We are honoured,' he said, bowing his head again, firmly tugging her hand down. Lyssa reluctantly bowed her head too. Phyleus may have been a prince, but she was a smuggler. Her manners were reserved for folk who didn't try to steal her crew members. 'This may save many other lives, along with those that they love,' he said, and closed his hand around the apple.

A familiar dazzling white flash engulfed her vision,

and when she blinked the light away Lyssa found herself somewhere she had only been once before: Zeus's throne room. She instinctively flexed her hand, confirming Phyleus's fingers were still entwined with her own, before looking around her.

A shout drew her attention to her right, where Hercules was slamming *Keravnos* into the shining marble floor, bellowing in rage. Hedone was sprawled a few feet from him, her hair and dress dishevelled and her skin covered in shallow scratches. She was breathing hard, tears rolling down her cheeks as she gazed imploringly at Hercules. Lyssa looked around quickly for Nestor, relieved to see the centaur uninjured on her left, a warhammer held tightly in each of her hands.

'Congratulations,' boomed Zeus's voice, and everyone's eyes snapped to the front of the room as the lord of the gods materialised on his throne. Zeus's throne room had no walls, just columns holding up a grand ceiling, and a panoramic view of the whole of Leo. It was at the very top of his palace, at the peak of Mount Olympus, and god-created wind whistled through the building. The floor, columns and huge throne were made from smooth marble and were all intricately carved with images of storms. Colour shimmered and rippled like light under the surface of the stone, making the carvings look surreally lifelike. Swirling silver clouds emitted blasts of violet and yellow lightning as Zeus lowered himself into the massive throne, and Lyssa dropped to one knee at the same time as Phyleus and Nestor did. Sparkling white light corkscrewed across the clouds on the floor beneath her, making her stomach lurch with disorientation.

'Captain Lyssa, you have gained a golden apple from my Hesperides. I am impressed,' Zeus rumbled, and Lyssa didn't dare raise her eyes to meet his. She straightened up, though, still clutching Phyleus's hand.

'Thank you, mighty Zeus,' she said. If he was as powerful as he claimed to be, then Zeus must be able to sense the roiling emotions that standing before him this way triggered inside her. The last time she had been here was when Hercules was pardoned for the murder of his family. Pardoned by *him*. Lyssa knew it wasn't wise to hate someone so powerful, and her own grandfather at that, but her seething anger was teetering on the edge of uncontrollable. Zeus had chosen Hercules as his hero and armed him with *Keravnos*. He was her enemy.

'Look at me, Captain Lyssa,' Zeus said, and cold dread filled her. She raised her eyes slowly to meet his. As she stared into them, she was surprised to see that they looked nothing like Hercules's cold grey ones. They were filled with life and power, sparking with violet energy. 'You have exceeded all expectations in these Trials, granddaughter,' he said softly. Lyssa heard a hiss from Hercules's direction, and felt a flash of smugness. 'You may keep the apple. It has no special properties, but it will be worth a fine sum of drachma. After all, I highly doubt there will be any others like it on the market.' A wicked grin flashed across his lips. 'You should be able to make some upgrades to that fine ship of yours.'

Lyssa's eyebrows flew up, her mouth dropping open. Zeus was praising the *Alastor*? Or was he mocking it? She blinked, and dipped her head again.

'Thank you. I am most grateful,' she stammered. She wasn't foolish enough to challenge him.

'Of course,' he said, his voice like silk. He paused a moment, his scrutiny almost unbearable, then straightened up on his throne. 'Heroes, Busiris is dead, and as such the *Orion* forfeits. The *Alastor* and the *Hybris* are the last two crews standing, and each have three wins. The last Trial will be hosted by my brother, Hades.' Zeus's beautiful face twisted into a snarl as Lyssa tried to process what he had just said. The *Orion* was out. 'Unfortunately, he is refusing to expose himself, or his precious Virgo, to Olympus. He wants his Trial to take place elsewhere. So, I have devised the last Trial for him.' A cruel grin danced across the god's lips. 'The first crew to kill the beast guarding the entrance to his realm will win the Trials. I will transport both of your ships to the entrance to Virgo in exactly one day's time.'

HADES

THE IMMORTALITY TRIALS

TRIAL TWELVE

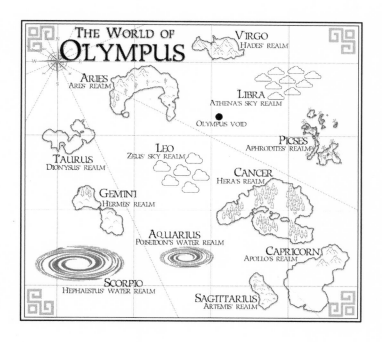

The World of Olympus

Virgo
Hades' realm

Aries
Ares' realm

Libra
Athena's sky realm

Olympus void

Taurus
Dionysus' realm

Leo
Zeus' sky realm

Picses
Aphrodite's realm

Gemini
Hermes' realm

Cancer
Hera's realm

Aquarius
Poseidon's water realm

Capricorn
Apollo's realm

Scorpio
Hephaestus' water realm

Sagittarius
Artemis' realm

1

LYSSA

The cheer that rose up when the white light faded and Lyssa found herself on the deck of the *Alastor* was deafening.

'You won! You won!' Len sang, beating Abderos and Epizon to the spot where she, Phyleus and Nestor had materialised on the planks, bouncing on his hooves.

'You aced it! I knew you would!' called Abderos, wheeling towards them quickly.

'Well done, Captain.' Epizon was stood behind him, beaming. Lyssa couldn't help flushing as her best friend's eyes flicked from her to Phyleus and back. Their hands were still locked together.

Lyssa's emotions tumbled over one another as she stared around at her smiling crew, adrenaline, love and passion merging and fizzing through her body. They *had* won. And more than that... Phyleus was hers.

'Cap, that apple... it's going to be worth a fortune,' Abderos said, his chair coming to a stop next to Len.

'The second golden apple to have ever left Zeus's

impossible-to-get-to secret garden? It's likely worth ten times what the ship is,' Phyleus said, turning to her.

'Nothing's worth ten times what the *Alastor* is.' Lyssa scowled at him and he laughed. The sound made her heart beat faster and her skin heat.

'I'm just talking drachmas here. Seriously. You're rich.' His deep brown eyes bored into hers and, try as she might, she couldn't bring herself care about drachmas.

'You mean we're rich,' snorted Len. 'Equal profit on this ship, I think you'll find. Except maybe the newcomers. Not sure how that'll work.' The satyr's words snapped Lyssa's attention away from Phyleus.

'Where are Evadne and Eryx?' she said, realising she couldn't see the 'newcomers'.

'Poseidon sent them to the *Orion*,' Epizon said into an awkward silence.

'Poseidon was here? On the *Alastor*?' Lyssa's heart began to hammer against her ribs in alarm. 'What about Tenebrae?'

'He just appeared, gave Eryx a longboat and told him to go and get the Hydra key he won in the second Trial,' said Abderos with a shrug. 'I saw it.'

'I don't think he was aware of Tenebrae. If he was, he didn't care or let on,' said Epizon.

'Athena said Eryx was important. Maybe the Hydra key was the reason,' said Lyssa, relieved that it seemed Tenebrae had evaded the god's detection. They already knew she could hide herself from Athena, but Poseidon? He was one of the three most powerful Olympians.

'Well, we've not got long to work out why,' said

Phyleus. 'Just a day until the last Trial.' The word 'last' cut through her torrent of thoughts, stilling them all.

'One more day and it's all over...' she breathed. This really was their final chance to stop Hercules.

'We're going to win this,' said Abderos. She looked at his grinning face, doubt and fear warring against her buoyant hope. There were two crews left. The Trials and Hercules had wiped everyone else out. And she had no doubt that the last Trial would be the most lethal yet. But reminding Abderos of that now was pointless. What harm could some positivity do them all now?

'Yeah? And what are you going to do with eternity?' she asked him.

'Build my own ship. The apple will help with that,' he said.

'I'm going to buy my way onto Pisces and surround myself with an endless supply of beautiful wood nymphs,' announced Len.

Nestor tutted behind him and Lyssa looked at her.

'What would you do with immortality, Nestor?' she asked.

'I don't age,' the centaur replied. 'So this is not a new concept for me. I will continue to serve Artemis as I always have planned to.' Lyssa nodded.

'I want to start another refuge on Libra for the home-less,' said Epizon. Lyssa knew of this plan, he'd told her about it before. 'Ab's right. The money from the apple will help a lot of us.'

'What about you, Cap?' asked Abderos.

'The farthest into the future I can think right now is being in my bath-tub in the next five minutes,' she lied, then started as she heard a shout from overhead. They all looked up to see a pale blue longboat descending towards the deck, Eryx leaning over the side.

When the little boat landed, Eryx leaped quickly from it, his face pale.

'Did you win?' he asked, breathlessly.

'Yes.' Lyssa nodded, and the big man's scarred face collapsed in relief as Phyleus held up the golden apple.

'So that bastard isn't immortal yet,' he said, releasing a long breath.

'Nope. Not yet.'

'Thank the gods. We got the Hydra key,' said Evadne, stepping out of the longboat. 'Did you talk to the Hesperides? Did the plan work?' She met Lyssa's eyes hopefully.

'Yes. You were right. We'd never have got past Ladon.' Lyssa paused, then said, 'Thank you. You're welcome on board the *Alastor* as long as you need to be here.'

Evadne smiled, a real, true smile that changed her face completely.

'I'll do whatever I can to help you stop him, Captain,' she said.

'Good.'

'I, um...' Eryx said, and she looked at him. 'Busiris is dead,' he said quietly, dropping his gaze to the planks. 'I... I didn't mean to kill him, but he would have killed Evadne, and...' He trailed off. Lyssa said nothing. Who was she to judge Eryx's actions? As far as she could tell, he was a far better man than Busiris had been. The guilt pouring from him confirmed it. 'Anyway,' the half-giant continued awkwardly. 'The *Orion* is empty. I thought you might find a use for it.'

Lyssa stared at him, her mouth falling open slightly. 'You don't want your own ship?'

Eryx shook his head.

'It wasn't my ship.'

'Whoa, whoa, whoa. You mean there's a Zephyr over there just floating about, up for grabs?' said Abderos, his voice disbelieving.

'Yes.'

Abderos gave a bark of laughter.

'Cap, now we're seriously rich.'

'Slow down, Ab. What would we do with a Zephyr? Eryx, it's a giants' ship. And you served your captain loyally. The *Orion* should belong to you.'

'That's what I think too,' said Evadne, reaching for the half-giant's hand. He dropped his gaze again, shifting his weight from foot to foot, the planks creaking under him.

'I don't know what to do with a ship,' he said quietly. 'I don't know how to be a captain. And besides, I want to be here, to help you kill Hercules.'

Respect and compassion for him swelled in Lyssa's heart. She had no doubt at all that Eryx was one of the good guys.

'Even more reason you deserve the *Orion*,' she said. 'Look, we'll do what we can to secure the *Orion* now, but if we survive this, then you need to consider the ship yours. Evadne will help you learn what you don't know.' She looked at the blue-haired girl.

'Of course I will,' she said. Eryx glanced sideways at her sceptically. 'How will you secure the *Orion*?' Evadne asked, turning back to Lyssa. 'I imagine the pirates are already on their way, given that the Trials are broadcast to the whole of Olympus. Unlike you, they're not going to turn down an opportunity to acquire an adrift Zephyr.'

'We can't tow it, it's far too big. And I'm not sparing a crew member,' Lyssa said, turning to Epizon. 'Reckon you can summon us up a little favour from our magic-wielding guest in the cargo deck?'

'I can ask her,' he said, and his eyes instantly unfocused. There was a flash of gold light, and the *Orion* suddenly appeared a hundred feet away from them, dwarfing the *Alastor*. The whole ship pulsed with the same gold glow for a few seconds, then the light faded. Evadne spluttered in shock and Eryx's mouth fell open.

'Man, she's good,' breathed Abderos, staring at the *Orion*.

Too good, thought Lyssa. No wonder she was sought after. What *was* she?

'The *Orion* will move with us; Tenebrae has created some sort of tether. But she wants light, Captain,' said Epizon, his eyes sharp again.

'She's earned it,' Lyssa said. 'Can you and Eryx manage her tank on your own?'

'Sure.' His eyes twinkled as they darted to Phyleus again. 'You get to that bath-tub,' he went on, the corner of his mouth quirking up slightly.

'I will,' she answered, willing the rising heat in her cheeks to cool. 'And we can talk about how much better your communication with Tenebrae has got later.'

'Sure thing, Captain.'

It was an effort of will to untangle her fingers from

Phyleus's, and Lyssa tried hard not to look into his eyes as she stepped towards the hauler.

'Five minutes,' Phyleus's voice sounded in her head. She kept her eyes on the hauler and her stride steady as her pulse began to race. 'I'll be at your door in five minutes.'

2

LYSSA

As soon as she entered her cabin Lyssa ran to the mirror in her washroom, anticipation fizzing through her body. She didn't just want Phyleus any more. She *needed* him. She needed to prove her love for him, to feel his in return. She watched her reflection, red curls falling around her face as she untied her headscarf. What did she need to do before he got here? She wasn't used to entertaining men; she didn't know what she was meant to do. She glanced down at her leather trousers and shirt. Was she supposed to be waiting for him on the bed, naked? That wasn't really her style. Nerves made her stomach flip as she looked around the little washroom, hoping for some inspiration. She *had* said she'd wanted a bath... She leaned over and turned the taps, warm water slowly beginning to fill the copper tub.

A knock at the door made her spin around quickly. Surely it hadn't been five minutes already?

'Who is it?' she called, half jogging to her door, heart pounding.

'It's me.' His voice sent a fresh wave of butterflies flitting through her stomach.

'You said five minutes!'

'I missed you. Three minutes is suddenly an unbearably long time.' He didn't expect her to do anything in particular, she realised with a rush. He just wanted to be with her. Her nerves melted away as she opened the door and looked into his intense brown eyes.

'Then you'd better come in.' She smiled.

'Are you actually running a bath?' he asked, stepping past her into her room.

'Yes.'

'Excellent,' he said, turning to face her. The heat in his gaze was enough to make all the muscles in her core clench. She kicked the door shut behind her as he wrapped his hands around the bottom of his shirt and pulled, revealing smooth, tanned skin, taut across his muscular stomach. Lyssa bit down on her bottom lip. 'I need a bath,' he said, dropping his shirt to the floor. His eyes were locked on hers as he took a step towards her.

'Me too,' she breathed, and then she was kissing him, her hands on his chest, his in her hair.

'I love you,' he said, sending the words through the ship, never breaking the intense hunger of his mouth on hers.

'I love you too,' she sent back fiercely, passion tearing through her as she pulled at the hem of her own shirt. His lips moved from her mouth to her jaw, then her neck, as he trailed kisses towards her open collar, and she gasped. Power roared through her body, her core aching and her skin alight with energy. He paused long enough

for her to pull her shirt over her head, and she heard his
ragged intake of breath as he saw her. Then his lips were
moving across her breasts and the *Alastor* lurched
beneath them.

'Phyleus,' she breathed. 'Phyleus, I don't know what
my power will do if I...' She floundered, looking for the
right words through her haze of lust. 'If I have a moment
of strong... release.'

He paused his kisses again, looking up at her with a
wicked gleam in his eyes.

'Then you're about to find out, Captain,' he said, and
she shrieked as he bent down, scooping her up into his
arms, and carried her into the washroom.

'I THINK the crew may have an idea of what we've been
doing,' Phyleus whispered into her ear, rousing her from
hazy sleep. She wiggled backwards, pushing herself
against his naked body, pressing as much of her own skin
against his as she could. A wave of contentment washed
over her.

'I don't care,' she mumbled. He pushed back against
her, and a little shudder of longing ran through her as
she felt his arousal.

'Really? You blush pretty easily, you know.'

'I'm captain. I can do what I like.'

'And I guess that includes flinging the ship all over
place whenever you're having a good time?' She rolled
over to face him, punching him in the arm.

'I'll get better at controlling it,' she said, looking into
his smiling face.

'Ahh, please don't. It doesn't do any harm to my reputation as a lover.' He grinned at her, and she punched him again. He laughed and kissed her, his warm hands moving down her back.

'I can't believe I held out on this so long,' she said, running her fingers along his jaw. 'You're amazing.'

'So are you,' he whispered. 'And it doesn't matter how long it took us to get here. We're here now.'

The thought of the real world, and the Trial they had yet to face, dampened Lyssa's bliss.

'What if this is the only time we get to do this? What if Hercules kills one or both of us tomorrow?' She couldn't help the trickle of fear that leaked into her words, and Phyleus pushed himself up on one elbow, cupping her cheek firmly in his other hand.

'Then we had something incredible before the end. I wouldn't have it any other way.' His warm gaze didn't flicker. He was fearless, Lyssa thought.

'How did you become so brave?'

Phyleus gave a little laugh.

'It was always cockiness and bravado, until you. Honestly, Lyssa, I would give anything for us, for you, to be free of Hercules tomorrow. But if today is all we have, then I wouldn't change a thing.'

'Nor would I,' she told him, and she meant it. But now that she knew what she could have if they won... The resolve and determination that had grown and grown over the last eleven Trials solidified inside her, everything she knew morphing into one truth. Only one crew would survive the twelfth Trial. And it would be them. Hercules must die.

'What would you do with eternity, Captain Lyssa?' Phyleus asked her softly. She stared into his face, the passion in his darkening eyes sending her pulse rocketing and her thoughts scattering.

'I don't give a damn about eternity,' she breathed, pressing herself against him. 'I just want you.'

3

HERCULES

When the flash of white light hit his chamber, Hercules tipped the last of the glass of ouzo down his throat with a snarl. He didn't know how much of the burning, clear spirit he had drunk. It was enough that he couldn't remember how the furniture had gotten so slashed up, the books and maps had been ripped apart, the broken glass had got everywhere. He had done it, he knew dimly. But he couldn't remember.

'You'll scare off that beautiful new prize of yours if you're not careful,' Zeus said, standing in the centre of the mess, looking around disdainfully. Hercules looked up at him from where he leaned against the mahogany wall, where the toppled bookcase had stood before. His head pounded angrily, and the sight of his father was filtered through a red haze. Zeus was appearing to him human-sized, but power rolled off his form as though he were larger than Olympus itself.

'You're here to tell me I'm a fool,' Hercules spat.

'Hercules, you are no fool. But you are allowing the rest of the world to see you as one.'

Rage bubbled under his skin, his muscles spasming as he sat up straight.

'I don't know what else I can do!' he shouted, banging his fist on the floor. 'They all have help! I have nothing!'

Purple electricity filtered through the red haze, crackling around his father.

'You have no help? What would you call assistance from the lord of the gods himself?' Zeus hissed, gesturing at *Keravnos* lying amongst the shredded remains of a couch. 'You are behaving like a spoiled child. You have the best ship, the best armour, the best weapon, the most strength and now you bed the goddess of pleasure. In what way, Hercules, do you believe you are at a disadvantage?' His voice had fallen to a deadly pitch, and a frisson of fear rippled through Hercules.

'I...'

'No more excuses!' Zeus bellowed, and power burst from him, booming through the *Hybris*. Hercules flinched as the windows at the back of his bedchamber shattered, the whole ship shaking. 'You will kill the beast tomorrow, and you will win immortality, or so help me, I will make you wish you had never been born! You will embarrass me no longer!' Sparks of electricity shot from Zeus's hands as he grew, his eyes becoming black and lethal. Hercules felt his whole body clench, control of his muscles abandoning him.

Fear took hold of him for real, the unfamiliar emotion overriding his anger and causing him to try to shrink back against the wall, struggling against the paralysis. Then, with a snarl, the god vanished in a flash of light.

Hercules sagged forward as his limbs came back to life, taking a long breath. Shame crept over him as he took long gulps of air, flexing his arms to reassure himself that they were working again. Zeus was right. He had everything he needed, and he was the strongest. Why hadn't he won already? He'd removed those he had believed were a threat, but that blasted girl was still clinging on, determined to make his life difficult. A vision of Megara, lying at his feet, covered in blood, forced its way past the image of Lyssa. She'd been trying to protect her son when he had killed her. *His son.* Hera had made him kill the child first, and he'd taken no pleasure in it. Would his son have been as strong as Lyssa had grown to be? He closed his eyes and shook his head. It didn't matter now.

Killing Megara had been different. She had deserved it. She had earned his wrath. A small bolt of power pulsed through his body. He was a force to be reckoned with, as he had proved time and time again. He thought about the lion he had killed in the first Trial, the sheer brute strength he had demonstrated to the world. He sat up straight, looking for the lion skin. For his trophy.

He spotted it lying on the floor, next to an armchair that was still intact, and pushed himself unsteadily to his feet to stumble towards it. His chest ached from where Evadne had embedded the crossbow bolt in it and his face twisted at the memory. Then the bolt he had fired into Hippolyta's gut came to mind, and a smile spread across his face as he replaced the image of Hippolyta with one of Evadne, blood spreading under her hands.

He dropped down into the armchair hard, and leaned over the side of it to scoop up the lion skin. The fur was still soft and thick, and he laid it on his lap, the empty lion eyes towards him. Gata had been beautiful as both a woman and a lion.

Another pulse of power shot through him at the thought. Red tinged the edges of his vision again as the urge to fight, to kill, roared up inside him. He gripped the lion skin hard. *Save it*, he told himself. *Save the rage for Hades' beast*. He could restore Zeus's faith in him. He had to.

The god's words rang in his head and he barely suppressed a shudder. How could he become as powerful as that? If he were immortal, he would be able to get closer to the gods. He would be able to gain favours, over time. He would learn their secrets. If he were immortal, he would have forever to grow in power and knowledge and influence. He would have forever to sate the constant, burning desire to destroy that Hera had unleashed when she made him kill his family. And he would have forever to work out how to become as powerful as Zeus.

4

HEDONE

A solitary tear slid down Hedone's cheek as Zeus's voice boomed through the *Hybris*. She closed her eyes, wrapping her arms tightly around her legs and taking a shaking breath as the ship rocked and vibrated around her. She thought she was in Evadne's old rooms, but she wasn't sure.

When Hercules had finally stopped drinking and stood up from his chair, she'd known from the look on his face that she couldn't make him feel better. His eyes were unfocused, his lips twisted, the man she loved nowhere to be seen in his vicious expression. She didn't think for a moment that he would harm her, but when he'd lifted *Keravnos* and brought it down through the middle of the couch she'd left the room quickly. Not knowing where to go, she picked a door she knew didn't lead to Asterion's rooms and slipped inside.

Hercules's temper took him to a place far, far away from her. She understood, of course, but that didn't stop her hating it. And now... Zeus's bellowed words had been clear. Hercules *had* to win the next Trial, or not only would he lose his chance of immortality and be humiliated in front of all of Olympus, but he would earn Zeus's wrath too. The pressure on him had already been great enough to affect him badly; how would he cope with this?

Hedone knew the answer to that, she told herself. He would fight. He would be strong. He would win.

And she had to help him. She had to make up for what had happened with Ladon. Exactly as Hercules had feared, she had become a hindrance rather than a help, getting captured and becoming a distraction. She clenched her teeth, regret rolling through her as thought about his stony demeanour when they had reappeared back on the *Hybris* deck at the end of the Trial. It was clear he was furious, with Zeus and Lyssa and at the loss of the Trial, but also with her. She'd apologised over and over as he said nothing. Eventually, with his fists clenched and his jaw twitching, he'd told her that he would fix it in the last Trial and had begun drinking.

Hedone knew she should stay out of his way. She knew he already loved her, that she didn't need to prove anything to him. But the thought of not being able to help him if he needed it was unbearable. And she knew that she couldn't help him defeat a beast. She wasn't a fighter, she wasn't strong. Her powers were useless, she couldn't seduce a monster.

Hedone took a long breath as the idea she'd being trying to squash and ignore for days took full hold of her. She knew what she could do to help him. And even though he wouldn't approve, she needed to show him how strong she could be.

5

ERYX

E ryx sat in the middle of the nest of sheets on the cargo deck, staring at Tenebrae. She stared back, unblinking. For the life of him, he couldn't imagine what kind of creature she was, to be able to fix the mast of the *Alastor* as she had, or how she had summoned and tethered the *Orion*.

'Eryx,' said a deep voice, and he swivelled around to see Epizon stepping out of the hauler.

'Epizon,' he said, pushing himself to his feet.

'Do you mind if I have an hour with Tenebrae?'

'Of course not,' Eryx said, leaning over to pick up his shirt. It was filthy and torn and he couldn't help the flicker of distaste that crossed his face as the smell of it hit him. 'Is there anywhere I can wash this?' he asked the first mate, holding it up. Epizon raised his eyebrows at the tattered garment.

'I think that shirt might be beyond washing. Why don't you take your new longboat over to the *Orion* and grab some wearable clothes?'

Eryx didn't want to go to the *Orion*. He didn't want to be on Antaeus's ship, where he'd just killed one of his own crew-mates. But he didn't want to tell Epizon that either.

'Um, yeah, sure. Good idea,' he mumbled, and walked towards the hauler.

'Eryx, you shouldn't blame yourself for what happened,' Epizon said quietly as they passed each other. 'Hercules is the only person to blame.'

'I killed Busiris. I knocked him overboard.'

'I spoke to Evadne. It sounds like Busiris had lost it. He was a cruel man and likely a killer too. You may have saved many more lives in the future, by causing the end of his.'

Eryx looked at Epizon's honest face.

'You think so?'

'Yes. I fought in the pits for years. I know of Busiris's reputation. And I recognise cruelty. You're no killer, Eryx.'

A small flurry of something like confidence rippled through Eryx as he processed the words. He knew Busiris had been cruel. And he knew that he himself had no desire to kill. Epizon was right. Antaeus had told him that Busiris was first mate because he had money. But he had never called him brother. And now the *Orion* was the last link Eryx had to his captain.

'I'll go and get some clothes from the *Orion*,' he said, nodding at Epizon. 'Thank you.'

'Sure. Maybe take Evadne with you, she's been obsessing over that Hydra key for hours. She could do with a break.'

Eryx smiled.

'Will do.'

EVADNE LEAPED at the chance to go to the *Orion* again. And when they landed on the deck, Eryx refused to let negative emotions overwhelm him. Instead, he concentrated on the good memories, and the kernel of hope that Hercules would pay for what he had done. They went straight to his rooms, where the sight of Evadne sitting cross-legged on his bed as he rummaged through his clothes drawers brought a smile to his face.

'Want to play dice?' he asked her.

'Dice? I have to work out how to open this stupid key,' she said, her eyebrows shooting up.

'We have about six hours until we reach Virgo. Just one game,' he coaxed. She cocked her head at him, a small smile on her lips.

'I thought you didn't want to come back here?' she asked. 'Now you want to stay and play dice?'

'I want to keep the good memories. And that includes learning to play dice with you, in my room.' Evadne's smile widened, her eyes lighting up.

'I get to go first,' she said.

He laughed.

'I'm the beginner, remember? Go easy on me.'

6

EVADNE

'Three Whirlwinds, I win!' Evadne threw her hands in the air triumphantly as she beamed down at the dice she'd just thrown.

'Best of five?' Eryx scowled at her. She opened her mouth to accept the challenge, but paused. Until they had begun to play games in Eryx's room, her mind had been dominated by fear. Busiris had made a good point, while she was strapped helpless to the mast of the ship. Hercules had a score to settle with her. If she went down to Virgo and he saw her... It would be a moment's work for him to kill her, if the opportunity arose. And if he won immortality... Killing her would be a mercy he would not show. He would make her suffer, she was sure. As nice as it was to escape reality for a short while, she was quite convinced that there was a good chance they were flying towards her death. She had to work out the Hydra key. Poseidon had said she could do it. Perhaps she could make a difference.

'We should get back to the *Alastor*,' she said. Eryx's face fell and she reached for him before she could stop herself. 'Thanks for the game, though.'

'Hmm. I don't think I was much of a challenge.'

'Then we'll have to play more, when this is over.'

'Do you... Do you think we'll win?'

'Yes,' Evadne said, firmly. 'We have to. Everyone on the *Alastor* has a good reason to want Hercules dead. And he is one man.'

'So... So we would become immortal?'

'I don't know if we would count as part of Lyssa's crew in the gods' eyes.' Evadne shrugged. It was strange to feel so indifferent towards the prize now. There was still the twinge of hope inside her, the familiar surge of longing when she thought about living forever, but it almost felt distant, like it was somewhere inside her, in a place she didn't access any more.

'If I was immortal, I could learn to become a really good captain,' said Eryx. Evadne laughed.

'You'll do that if you only live to eighty,' she told him. He looked at her seriously.

'And you'll help me?'

'Always.'

A flash of indecision crossed his broad face, then he leaned forward and kissed her. It was a brief, awkward kiss, his face that much larger than hers, his movements unsure and clumsy, but it made her heart soar and her breath catch. He moved backwards quickly, his face aflame.

'I, um, I...' he started, but she held her hand up to his

lips, silencing him. Then she leaned forward, and kissed him gently.

She didn't know if they were going to beat Hercules. Truth be told, she couldn't imagine how anything could stop him, when the bloodlust took him. But she knew that as long as she was with Eryx, and he was happy, she had made all the right decisions.

BUT A FEW HOURS later Evadne was no closer to working out the Hydra key, and she couldn't help her mounting anxiety as she stood with the crew of the *Alastor* on the top deck. The dark metal of the key was warm, from being held in her sweating palms. She'd spent hours now, examining the surface for hidden seams or joins, scouring the intricate pattern carved in it for clues or holes or mistakes. But she could see nothing. It was just a solid metal sphere.

She tried to slow her thumping heart as Lyssa strode onto the deck. The captain was dressed as she usually was in leather trousers and boots, and a white shirt. A weapons belt was strapped across her hips and loaded with slingshots and a dagger, and her red curls were pushed back from her face by her headscarf. But despite her diminutive stature, nobody stood before her at that moment would doubt she had Zeus's power flowing through her veins. She was emanating power, Evadne thought, hope blossoming. She'd never felt power like this from Lyssa before, even though she had seen her use her Rage. This was something else. And it was so *different* to Hercules's power. His seethed and flowed and grew, like expanding shadows. Lyssa's pulsed and bounced and danced, like the light on the sails of her ship.

Was it to be that simple at the end? Light versus dark? The contrast seemed so clear, so stark now, that Evadne couldn't understand how she had ever been on the wrong side.

7

LYSSA

Lyssa felt as though she could barely contain the power flooding her body as she stepped onto the top deck. She didn't know whether it was the overwhelming emotions for Phyleus charging her power, or her new connection with the *Alastor*, but she was grateful for it.

'This is it,' she said loudly, the eyes of every crew member on her. 'This is our last chance to stop that evil bastard once and for all. Anyone who wants to fight can come. But make no mistake, you will not just be facing Hades' monster. Hercules may try to kill you.'

'That's if he's not *already* trying to kill you,' said Len, with a nervous grin.

Lyssa gave him a sideways look.

'True. But if we're all dead, he has no competition and he wins by default. It's a valid strategy that we know he would use; look at what he did to the hippocampus on Aquarius.'

'Should we be using the same strategy?' asked Nestor.

'Absolutely not. I, for one, have no desire to kill Hedone, or the minotaur for that matter,' said Lyssa. 'I just want Hercules dead. If you come, you must follow my orders when given. And I will not hold it against anybody if they want to stay here.'

EVERYBODY WANTED TO FIGHT. The look on Abderos's face when Lyssa told him she needed him on the ship pained her.

'Ab, I'm sorry, I truly am, but it's just not going to work. Plus, what if we need a lift out? You saved mine and Epizon's life on Scorpio and Aquarius.' He screwed his face up, and for a moment he looked as young as he was, before giving a big sigh.

'Fine. If anyone needs rescuing, I'll be here,' he said resignedly.

'Thank you,' she said, and leaned over to hug him. He let out a small huff in response.

'Captain,' Eryx said behind her, and she straightened up and turned to the half-giant. 'I'd like to help you fight Hercules,' he said quickly. 'I don't care about immortality, I just want him dead.'

'As do I,' said Nestor from her other side. Lyssa thought about it. If she, Nestor and Eryx took on Hercules, surely he wouldn't stand a chance?

'If Hercules kills whatever's guarding the gates of Virgo before us, then it's all over anyway,' Len said, and she looked down at the little satyr. 'Someone has to fight it.'

He had a point.

'I'll help, if I can,' said Evadne.

'Can you fight?'

'Not really. But I can shoot.'

'Good. Look, we don't know what we're facing, or what Hercules will try to do. Just follow my orders and do your best,' Lyssa said, and everyone around her nodded.

'Captain, can I talk to you before we get there?' Epizon's concerned voice sounded in her head and her eyes snapped to his. His face was creased with worry.

'Of course,' she answered, and made her way to the hauler. 'Cargo deck?'

HE WAS THERE a moment after her, and strode immediately towards Tenebrae's tank. As he reached it he held his hand to the glass and she flitted effortlessly through the liquid, placing her own palm against his. There were shining, delicate webs between her fingers.

'She really, really doesn't want to go to Virgo,' he said, and as he turned back to her, Lyssa could see tears shining in his eyes. 'She's scared, and I don't know how to help her,' he half whispered.

'Oh, Ep.' Lyssa moved to his side quickly. 'We *have* to go. You know we do. If we let Hercules win, he'll keep killing for eternity.'

'I know. I know we have to go. And she knows too.'

'If she could sort Hercules out for us, then we wouldn't have to,' Lyssa said, only half-joking. Epizon looked seriously at her.

'Hercules is protected from magical influences.'

'What?'

'She's already tried. I didn't ask her to, but we've been talking a lot and when she understood that it was him who had nearly killed me and how much I hate him for what he's done to you...' Epizon turned back to Tenebrae, and she ducked in the liquid, bringing her face close to their hands. 'She couldn't reach him. She thinks it may be *Keravnos*, blocking the magic.'

'Right. Well, um.' Lyssa looked at Tenebrae. 'Thanks very much for trying,' she told her. The creature's gaze flicked to hers for a moment, then settled back on Epizon's face.

'Captain, I have to protect her. From whatever she's scared of.'

'Do you want to stay with her instead of coming down to Virgo?' Lyssa asked him, praying the answer was no. She needed him. Not just for his fighting skill. He was her best friend and first mate. She couldn't imagine making her final stand without him.

'No. Of course not. We have to stop Hercules.' Lyssa said a million silent 'thank you's and was sure Tenebrae's gaze flicked to hers again.

'OK. Why won't she tell you what she's afraid of? Do you think it's Hades?'

'I don't know. I think she's trying to protect me.'

Unease rolled through Lyssa.

'I'm not sure even Tenebrae can protect you from a god,' she said. This time the creature's eyes definitely met Lyssa's. 'No offence,' she said quickly, holding her hands up. Epizon looked at her. 'What do you want me to do, Ep?' she asked him.

He let out a long sigh.

'Nothing. I guess I just wanted you to know that I want to help her. If we can.'

'OK. If there's anything we can do, we will. I promise.'

8

LYSSA

'Are you ready for this?' Phyleus asked Lyssa as she leaned over the railings, watching the sparkling lilac clouds roll past them.

'Yes,' she said, turning to him. 'Are you?'

'Nope. Not even a little bit.' He grinned at her, then stepped close, wrapping his arms around her waist. She felt a flash of worry that the rest of the crew would see them, then remembered that they probably all knew that she and Phyleus were together anyway. And even if they didn't, what difference did it make now? She stood on tiptoes and kissed him.

'Then you'd better get ready,' she said.

'Lyssa, please don't do anything rash or...'

'Stupid?' she finished for him. 'I told you it would be weird if we were nice to each other. Now you won't call me stupid.'

'I mean it,' he said, rolling his eyes. 'Hercules is dangerous.'

Annoyance flared inside her.

'You think I don't know that? Don't you dare start treating me like a child now,' she snapped, pushing back from him.

'No, no, that's not what I meant! I meant... You're brimming with power. Like, it's practically pouring off you. I'm worried you'll get cocky.'

She scowled at him.

'Surely this is the exact time to get cocky. I'm stronger than I've ever been, and you can obviously feel that too.'

'It's *his* power inside you, Lyssa, remember that. You've seen how it affects him, how far it's taken him. Cocky leads to stupid. Or worse.'

'But my power is different, it's not just Rage any more,' she protested.

He raised an eyebrow.

'Really?'

'I think so.'

'All the same, you mustn't lose control or let it overtake you.'

'But when I had *Keravnos*, on Pisces, I nearly killed him. I had enough strength, enough power. Letting it take over helped me, made me better.'

'Would you have stopped there?' he asked her, gently. She dropped her gaze. She'd told Epizon about what she'd felt that night, but not him. How she knew she wouldn't have stopped with Hercules. 'You weren't yourself, Lyssa. The look in your eyes, the fury on your face... It wasn't you.'

'Does it matter, if it gets the job done? Does it matter how my strength is fuelled if we need it to win?'

'No, as long as you can live with whatever happens next.'

'Nothing will happen next if we lose!' she shot back. 'We'll all die.'

'I just...' He pushed his hand through his hair, frustrated. 'If you feel like you're losing control, I'll be there,' he said eventually, looking back at her. 'I'll be wherever you are.'

'The best way you can help me is to not get yourself killed,' she said softly.

'Fine. I'll do that.' He kissed her again, and there was a flash of bright white light.

IT WAS INSTANTLY COLDER, and the sky around the ship was no longer sparkling with clouds. Instead, the light was tinged a dull orange and nothing moved. Lyssa spun quickly around, leaning over the railings, and letting out a slow breath at the view below. The island was close, barely more than a hundred feet down, rocky brown mountains stretching up almost as high as the ship. The land was utterly barren. Not a single tree or plant or creature was in sight. But at the base of the nearest mountain yawned a huge black cave mouth. Lyssa's stomach flipped as she stared at it.

'Look,' said Phyleus quietly, and she straightened up, following his pointing finger. The *Hybris* was opposite them, its metal-clad hull reflecting the muddy light.

'Take us down, Ab.' She sent the thought to her navigator as she saw the longboat rise from Hercules's ship. The *Hybris* was too big to land in front of the cave, but her ship wasn't. The *Alastor* would carry them to the gates of hell, for their final battle.

9

LYSSA

Hercules, clad in his lion skin and flanked by the minotaur and Hedone, disappeared into the pitch blackness of the cave mouth as Lyssa stepped out of the hauler, onto the dusty rock of Virgo.

'We must hurry, Captain; we don't want him to get too far ahead,' said Nestor, her tail flicking and her expression severe as she trotted past them.

'Right,' Lyssa replied, trying to force down her mounting anxiety. She felt like a coiled spring, adrenaline and pent-up power making her head spin and her breaths shorten. Phyleus gripped her hand as they walked swiftly towards the gaping darkness and she squeezed back, trying to stop her hand shaking.

'We're going to end this today, Captain,' said Epizon beside her, as they reached the cave mouth. She tore her eyes from the inky nothingness to stare at his reassuring face.

'No more running,' she said. 'Ever.'

'No more running,' he repeated, and they stepped into the dark.

LYSSA DIDN'T THINK she had ever experienced such darkness. She tried to force her legs forward but fear of what could be in front of her pinned her feet to the rock. Phyleus was motionless beside her, his hand still clasped around hers.

'Cap?' came Len's voice, tiny in the blackness.

'Stay where you are,' she said sharply. 'Hercules and his crew are in here somewhere, along with Olympus knows what else.'

They waited in silence, seconds feeling like hours as Lyssa prayed their eyes would adjust, but the dark was endless and unrelenting. With her eyesight taken away Lyssa felt vulnerable and on edge. The very air around them became menacing and oppressive.

'Can you hear me?' she sent the thought Phyleus.

'Yes,' he answered instantly. Some of her rising panic ebbed a bit at his voice.

'What do we do?'

'It's too dangerous to move,' Phyleus said aloud. 'There could be a cliff edge in front of us for all we know.'

'I agree,' said Nestor, and Lyssa turned towards her voice. Suddenly blue light flickered to life around them, and Lyssa almost choked in relief as the suffocating darkness receded, shapes and shadows forming around them. They were in a huge cavern, the ceiling high above them and covered in long, sharp stalactites. The light was coming from a river that wound through the cavern ahead of them, disappearing out of sight around a bend at the back of the cave. As they watched, the light of the river grew into a brilliant blue, and smoke or steam seemed to roll off its surface.

'Movement, Captain,' said Epizon and pointed. A boat was travelling along the river towards the middle of the cavern, a dark stooped figure pushing it along with a pole. He came to a stop, and his hooded head slowly lifted towards them.

'What do we do now?' Eryx's voice was loud in the cavern, and Lyssa jumped.

'He's the ferryman. He'll take us to the underworld,' said Phyleus.

'How'd you know that?' Len looked up at him in surprise.

'I've... been here before.' His face was as serious as Lyssa had ever seen it.

'You've taken part in the Elysium Mysteries?' Evadne breathed. He nodded.

'What are they?' Eryx asked.

'We'll discuss it later,' said Lyssa quickly. 'We need to go.'

THEY ALL MOVED QUICKLY across the uneven ground towards the boat, the ferryman's face remaining cloaked in darkness despite the light around him.

'I am Charon,' he said, when Lyssa was a foot away from the glowing river's edge. His voice was scratchy and high and made Lyssa's face twitch. She resisted the urge to cover her ears. 'You must pay for your crossing. There are six of you, so the cost will be high.'

'We have drachma, on our ship,' Lyssa said. Charon chuckled and the sound made Lyssa feel queasy.

'I only take gold from the dead. If you expect to leave Virgo, you must each sacrifice someone you hold dear. If you are not willing to part with anybody now, a life from your future will suffice.'

Lyssa gaped at him.

'What? No!'

'I don't think so, Charon,' Phyleus said, and the hooded figure turned to him. He was standing tall, his chin pushed out and his eyes narrowed, looking and sounding every bit the prince he was. 'I believe I can claim crossing for everybody here,' he said.

Charon leaned forward slowly, and Lyssa heard his long, raspy breaths. Two skeletal hands crept out of the dark cloak, and to her horror, he pushed back his hood.

The ferryman was like something straight out of one of Lyssa's nightmares, and she stumbled backwards as the hood fell away. Torn bits of flesh clung to his mostly exposed skull, showing starkly red in the blue light. His jaw hung from his face unnaturally, his gaping mouth filled with squirming maggots. Where his eyes should have been were two black pits that were somehow even more disturbing than their rotten surroundings.

'You have survived the Mysteries,' he hissed, after staring into Phyleus's face for a long moment.

'Yes. And as such, have unlimited access to Virgo.'

'Those you bring with you do not,' Charon said.

'They are my family. The honour extends to them.'

'Family...' Charon mused. 'It is true that the rites extend to family...' He turned his hideous face to cast his glance over each of them. Only Nestor held his gaze without flinching or shrinking away and Lyssa's respect for the fierce centaur deepened. 'You may board,' Charon said eventually, and mercifully reached for his hood once more. The little boat expanded as they stepped forward, becoming large enough to carry them all.

Lyssa climbed in first, her heart hammering as she moved past Charon.

'You didn't tell me you had unlimited access to Virgo,' she said to Phyleus, mentally.

'I had no intention of ever coming back here. And as the gods set the Trial here, I thought we'd bypass the river Styx.'

'I wonder what Hercules paid,' said Epizon, as he climbed in.

'A life is no payment for a killer,' Charon said. 'Hercules had to pay with something more dear to him than that.'

Lyssa looked at the ferryman. 'What was it?'

He pointed towards the river. Lyssa leaned out to follow his gnarled hand and gasped. The river wasn't liquid at all. It looked like the clouds they flew through every day, glowing eerily, with shimmers whirling through it like currents. And there, floating and spinning gently, was *Keravnos*, its red glow turning purple in the blue light.

'He gave up *Keravnos*,' she breathed.

'It was that or stay on the banks of the Styx,' Charon said, then the boat lurched forward and began to follow the winding river through the cavern. Lyssa said nothing, apprehension tightening every muscle in her body as they approached the bend.

'Do you know what Hades' beast is?' she asked Phyleus, knowing he would already have told her if he did.

'No. Charon rendered me unconscious before we left the banks,' he said, with a sideways glare at the ferryman.

'Some secrets must be kept,' Charon replied grimly.

'This is being shown to the whole of Olympus,' said Eryx.

'A travesty,' rasped Charon.' What you are about to see has been forbidden to the living for thousands of years. And it should stay that way.' The boat lurched as the ferryman's voice rose.

'OK, OK, we get it,' said Len quickly. 'We'll be out of here as soon as we can.'

Charon hissed but said nothing, and a moment later they rounded the corner.

Posted at the gates is Cerberus, a huge hound with three massive heads. He is a savage and monstrous beast with a thunderous bark, who constantly guards the halls of Hades and Persephone with his fearsome menaces.

EXCERPT FROM

THE GOLDEN ASS BY APULEIUS

Written 2 AD

Paraphrased by Eliza Raine

10

HEDONE

Hedone's hands and feet felt numb as she gaped at the gates in front of her. The actual gates themselves were made from iron bars wider than she was, and were at least forty feet high. Towering over them was an iron statue of a demon, its eyes burning scarlet.

Stretching out from either side of the demon and around the gates were massive wings that ran all the way down the long chamber they were standing in, forming walls that went up a hundred feet. Thick bones ran up the wings at intervals, like ribs, and the sections between were slightly see-through, like membrane. Hedone could see red and orange light moving through them, like mighty flames burning on the other side. She could smell smoke, and was sure the cavern was getting hotter as they approached the gates.

'Is that the beast?' she whispered, resisting the urge to clutch Hercules's arm.

'No,' he muttered, his voice quiet in the silent cavern. He was unarmed, *Keravnos* now lost to the river Styx, but his fists were clenched as he strode ahead. Asterion's hooves clicked on the black stone beneath them.

'They are here, Captain,' the minotaur said, and Hedone glanced backwards, first seeing the large form of Eryx, then making out Epizon, Lyssa, Phyleus, the centaur and the little satyr.

A low growl began to rumble across the room, starting behind the gates and rippling along the wing walls. Hercules stopped, looking around as the growl grew louder and louder.

'When the fighting starts, move back,' he told Hedone, pointing where they'd come from, the faint blue glow of the Styx still just visible behind the approaching crew of the *Alastor*. 'Stay out of the way and don't come anywhere near whatever this is. Do you understand?' He had to shout the last words over the roar that was now reverberating through the cavern.

'Yes,' she shouted back, nodding. He leaned forward and kissed her, hard, then turned back to the gates, dropping his stance. Hedone turned and jogged towards one of the wings, feeling the heat rise as she got closer. Keeping a safe distance from the strange wall she turned back to the cavern, where Lyssa was running now, only ten feet from Hercules. Then a crashing thump drew everyone's attention back to the gates, and fear paralysed Hedone instantly, her legs turning to jelly beneath her.

The beast that had appeared in front of the gates was on fire. Flames licked up from its black fur, and Hedone let out a small whimper as all three of its heads snapped towards Hercules. She forced herself to look at the thing long enough for her eyes to adjust, until she could see more than just teeth through the searing flames. It looked like a huge wolf, about three times the size of Hercules, who was now crouched in front of it, his lion skin wrapped around him, and Asterion to his left. Its eyes were deeper red than the fire covering its body, and they were slanted and angular, like gemstones. Something dark dripped from all three of its huge jaws as they snapped and snarled.

Hedone had seen many monsters during the Immortality Trials, most of them larger than this creature, but none had scared her so much. Its presence induced a fear in her so bone-deep that she wanted to run and run and never stop.

'This is my guard-dog, Cerberus.' A voice echoed around them. 'He is bound to the gates, and will not give chase, should you decide to flee. But defeat him and you will win the Immortality Trials.'

Hedone dropped weakly to her knees as Cerberus began to howl.

11

HERCULES

Hercules whirled around as Asterion shouted, tearing his eyes from the flaming beast in front of him just as Lyssa barrelled into him. He flew backwards, rolling to his side fast as he skidded towards Cerberus.

The creature lunged forward on his muscular haunches, jaws snapping, but Hercules was too fast. The guard-dog didn't follow him as he raced back towards Lyssa, who was now facing him with a dagger in both hands. Epizon was to her right, a machete raised high above his head, and the prince from Taurus was on her left, aiming a loaded slingshot. The last living member of the *Orion* crew, Eryx, was dancing on the balls of his feet, his raised fists clenched, and the white centaur galloped to a stop at her side, wielding two warhammers. Weapons were strapped all over her torso. Hercules barked a laugh as he slowed to a stop before them.

'You see what you need to match my strength?' he shouted at his daughter. 'You need an army!' He laughed again, loudly, genuinely delighted. The girl had to bring every fighter she could find to stand even a chance against him. And he knew, as hatred and rage and desire flooded through his body, that he would win.

Her red hair blurred as she glared at him, and the fiery light tingeing the cavern and glowing through the walls mingled with the red that was seeping into his eyes. The growl of the beast behind him dimmed as blood pounded through his ears, adrenaline flooding through him. Cerberus would guard the gates, and no more. He had plenty of time to finish what he had started with his daughter. And he would incapacitate her, not kill her. A quick death was too good for her. She needed to watch as he ripped the guts from the half-giant. She needed to see him break the centaur's legs. She had to bear witness as he removed her first mate's head with his own machete. And she would be helpless as he clubbed the prince to death, as he had her mother and brother. Hercules needed to see her pain, hear her sobs, watch her break. He needed to show his father what happened to people who made a fool of him. *He needed to erase what was left of Megara, and her family.*

And when he was finished with Lyssa, and he had killed the drooling beast behind him, he would find Evadne and he would keep her alive as long as he possibly could. He would pick apart both her body and her mind until she was nothing but a shell of her disobedient self. He would make her pay for betraying him. He would make her beg for death every minute of every day, and never relent, and then what was left of her would age and wither, while he stayed young and vigorous for eternity.

'They're all here to fight Cerberus,' Lyssa called. 'I'm here to fight you.'

A thrill thundered through Hercules's body, and he felt his muscles expand. 'Asterion, don't let them kill the beast,' he hissed, without taking his eyes off his daughter. Then with a roar, he charged.

12

LYSSA

Lyssa began to run towards Hercules, preparing herself to jump at the last moment. Power and energy flowed through her and she knew she was as ready as she would ever be. Then a flash of white light engulfed her vision and she felt her body freeze. She gave a shout of frustration as her eyes were forced closed against the light. What was happening? Why was a god getting involved now?

When she opened her eyes she was standing in a different room. Cerberus, Hercules and the fiery wings were nowhere to be seen. This was a throne room, she realised as she looked around her quickly, adrenaline still making her limbs shake, still ready to fight. Phyleus was next to her, and Epizon was there too, both men looking equally confused as they blinked in the dark room. It was circular, and every surface was made from a black, shining stone that sparkled with pinpricks of light. A throne on one side of the room was raised ten feet off the ground, simple and angular, and rows of benches carved

from the same black stone lined the rest of the chamber.
It could easily fit a few hundred people, Lyssa thought.

'This is Hades' throne room,' Phyleus whispered, and
Lyssa's heart skipped a beat.

'Why are we here?'

'I don't know.'

'I do,' said Epizon, and she spun around to look at
him, his face pale.

'You all do,' a voice said, and it was like no voice Lyssa
had ever heard. It was as though it had actually slithered
into her ears, and her fingers flew to them immediately,
rubbing and scratching at them, trying to remove the
alien feeling. The others were doing the same around
her, Phyleus's face contorting with disgust. 'Give me what
I need, and you may re-join the Trial. Hand her over.'

'Hand who over?' shouted Lyssa, her Rage building as
the awful feeling crawled further inside her head. 'Get
out!' she shouted, pulling at her ears now, the feeling
reaching the back of her throat, making her gag.

'Hades, show yourself if you want to talk!' Phyleus
bellowed, and suddenly the feeling vanished. Lyssa
gulped down air, shaking her head as black smoke began
to fill the room. Slowly, it solidified into a humanoid
shape, standing in front of the throne.

'You're much more forceful than you were when you
came here before, young prince,' the smoke being said,
its slithering voice gone, replaced by a cool, calm tone. In
the same way that power rolled off Zeus and Poseidon,
darkness and cold emanated from Hades. The tendrils of
smoke dancing away from his body towards them set
Lyssa shuddering in uncontrollable fear.

'I can thank your Mysteries for that, Hades,' replied Phyleus, and he bowed low. Lyssa and Epizon followed suit.

'The Mysteries will seem like a child's game compared to what I will put you all through if you don't hand over the being. I know she is on your ship.'

'We don't know what you're talking about,' Lyssa said, glaring at the smoke. More tendrils curled towards her, and as they got closer screams began to sound deep in her mind. Visions flashed before her eyes, men stretched over torture racks, blades falling across necks, hollow, empty eyes staring at her. 'Stop it!'

'Then show me some respect,' Hades hissed, and Lyssa couldn't help stumbling backwards, the terror his voice instilled in her was so real.

'We will never hand her over,' Epizon said, stepping towards Hades.

'Ep—' Lyssa started, but he cut her off.

'He knows she's there, Captain. There is no point lying.'

'Clever young man,' Hades said. 'I am afraid she has become rather attached to you, and your ship. She doesn't seem to want to leave.'

'So let her be.'

Lyssa's mouth fell open as Epizon raised his chin. What was he doing speaking to the god of the underworld like that?

'I don't want to hurt her,' Hades said, and Lyssa was surprised at the softness in his voice. 'I want to help her.'

'It doesn't look much like that from here,' she said. 'Besides, we have no power over her. If she can resist the will of a god, what do you think we can do about it? I need to get back to Hercules and Cerberus, now.'

'Not until I have the being.' The smoke form turned to Epizon. 'Call her here.'

'No.' Epizon didn't hesitate to say the word... Then he crumpled to the floor, throwing his hands over his ears and screaming.

'Stop! Please, stop!' shouted Lyssa, dropping down beside him. Epizon's screams turned to whimpers, and he curled up on the stone. 'We can't control her, we've told you!' she shouted again, fury rolling through her as she reached for Epizon.

'He can,' Hades said, and Epizon's screams began again, louder than before. Tears of anger and frustration filled Lyssa's eyes as she gripped the big man's shaking shoulders.

'Please, please stop,' Phyleus called, dropping down beside her.

'I don't want to hurt—' Hades started, but purple light filled the air, and a blast of energy burst out from the middle of the throne room, cutting him off. Epizon's screams ceased as Lyssa gaped at the source of the blast. A bubble was hovering five feet above the stone, and in the middle of it, eyes fixed on Hades, was Tenebrae.

13

LYSSA

Epizon pushed himself up suddenly, breaking Lyssa's transfixed stare.

'Ep, are you OK?'

'She shouldn't be here,' he said quickly, struggling out of Lyssa's grip and to his feet. 'Tenebrae, leave now!'

Her bubble turned with her as she faced him, her intense eyes softening a little.

'I'm sorry to draw you out like that,' Hades said, the ice in his voice gone. 'You have grown to be truly magnificent. And you are called Tenebrae?' The bubble moved, and she faced Hades once more. 'I really mean you no harm. In fact, I have found you sanctuary. I have a found a god strong enough and willing to keep you safe.'

'She's safe on the *Alastor*,' barked Epizon.

'Not as safe as she could be. And would you really have her kept in a tank in the dark her whole life? I can offer her a world she was meant to live in. A world where she can become everything she was meant to be.'

'Meant to be?' Epizon said, then his expression

changed, his eyes becoming vacant, as they did when Tenebrae was communicating with him. 'You...' he whispered, after a few seconds. 'You created her?'

Hades paused, then nodded, the smoke shifting as he moved.

'Yes. To live in a thirteenth realm.'

Lyssa couldn't help the gasp that escaped her lips, and Phyleus spluttered in surprise.

'Creating a new realm broke many of our rules, and Zeus punished me as he saw fit. He destroyed the realm I'd worked so long and hard to create, and every new creature in it.'

'Except Tenebrae.'

'Except Tenebrae. I managed to get her out. But I disguised her so well she was stolen, by fools who had no idea how important, or powerful, she was. Zeus and the others will not let her live if they find her.'

'Where do you want to hide her?'

'I can't tell you that.' Another burst of power pulsed from Tenebrae's bubble and Hades let out a long sigh. 'Telling you could mean your death, if the other gods discover that you know.'

'Fine,' said Lyssa.

'Things are changing in Olympus. An ancient and powerful force has recently awoken. A force with greater power than any of the gods.'

'How is that possible?'

'A Titan,' breathed Phyleus. The smoky form of Hades turned to look at him.

'Indeed. And all gods need a realm. No matter Zeus's feelings, a thirteenth realm will exist before long. And I have bargained for her sanctuary there. If she wishes it, she will live like a queen, and her powers will blossom. She could be the greatest creature ever known to Olympus.'

'Epizon, if he's telling the truth then we should consider this.' Lyssa looked up at her first mate. His eyes were filled with glistening tears. 'Epizon?'

'She will only go if he goes with her. She is in love with him,' Hades said eventually, in a quiet voice. Lyssa looked between the god and Epizon, pain blossoming in her chest as the tears began to roll down Epizon's cheeks and she realised what was coming.

'And you're in love with her,' she whispered.

'I'm sorry, Lyssa. I can't leave her.'

'You will be a king,' Hades said, and Lyssa turned to him, glaring, her head spinning. She couldn't deal with this now. Not when they were so close.

'Send us back to the Trial, now! We can deal with this afterwards, if we survive!'

'That's exactly why I cannot do that. If Epizon is killed, I don't know what Tenebrae would do.' The bubble pulsed gently at his words, and Tenebrae's eyes were fixed on Epizon. 'And when this Trial is complete, all the gods of Olympus will convene. She may be as powerful as one god, but she could not manage them all. I need to get her to safety now.'

'No...' Lyssa put her face in her hands, her mind refusing to accept what was happening. 'Ep, I can't lose you,' she said desperately, grabbing his arm with both of her hands. 'I need you on the *Alastor*, I need you as my first mate.' Tears burned in her eyes as her voice broke. 'You're my best friend.'

'I'm sorry, Lyssa,' he whispered back, his face wet. 'I'm sorry. But I love her.' She threw her arms around him and let the tears come as he gripped her. 'You have Phyleus now, he'll give you more than I ever did,' he said into her hair.

'It's not the same,' she sobbed.

'I know. But we'll still be able to talk. And I'm sure you can visit?'

'The *Alastor* will be granted rights to come and go as you please, I swear,' said Hades.

'Are you sure, Epizon? You're sure you want to do this?'

'Yes,' he said, and gripped her shoulders, holding her at arm's length so that he could look into her face. 'You need to be out there, stopping Hercules, for the sake of all Olympus. I'll be fine. Better than fine. I'll be happy. This is what I want.' Lyssa stared up at him, unable to picture life on her ship without him, unable to face letting him go.

'Lyssa, I'm sorry, but... we have to go. Or this all becomes irrelevant,' Phyleus said quietly from behind her.

'Go, Captain,' Epizon said, straightening up. 'Go and save Olympus. I'll see you when you're immortal.'

'I love you, Ep,' Lyssa whispered, and he held her to his chest.

'I know. I love you too.'

'Thanks for everything,' Phyleus said, stepping forward as Epizon let go of her. Epizon shook Phyleus's outstretched hand. Lyssa took a shaky gulp, trying to control her sobs, when purple filled her vision, and she was suddenly standing in the endless room of columns again.

'Tenebrae?' she said, whirling around on the spot. 'What the...?' She jumped as she suddenly felt something solid in her hand, and looked down. It was a bow, made from the palest wood, with strings of some material that glowed a faint violet. As she frowned at it, the columns began to shimmer, and then she was back in Hades' throne room, still clutching the beautiful bow.

'Tenebrae says thank you.' Epizon smiled.

'As do I,' said Hades.

'Good luck, Captain,' Epizon said, and the world flashed white once again.

14

EVADNE

Evadne stood fifty feet from the glowing blue river, gripping the Hydra key so hard her hand hurt. Lyssa, Phyleus and Epizon had just disappeared. Vanished into thin air as Hercules launched himself at Lyssa.

Nestor had been the only one not to lose her head in the moment of confusion, galloping towards Hercules with her hammers shining in the fiery light. The first one hit him, but glanced harmlessly off his lion skin. The second went wide as he spun and rolled out of the centaur's path. Eryx had bellowed then, sprinting into the fight.

Cerberus, the enormous, burning mass of teeth and muscle, was prowling back and forth in front of the demon gates, snapping whenever Asterion got close to him. The minotaur was wielding a lethal-looking spiked mace, but it seemed to barely be bothering the monster, and Eryx and Nestor's attentions were fixed on Hercules.

Where was Hedone? Evadne scanned the narrow room and spotted her crouching by one of the wings that made up the walls of the cavern. She was too far away for her face to show clearly, but she wasn't moving. Evadne guessed she was in the grip of the same barrage of fear she was experiencing herself. *Pull yourself together, Evadne*, she told herself, gritting her teeth. *You may not be a fighter, but they need you. Work out what the damn key is for.*

She glared down at the metal orb, and realised with a stab of surprise that the glowing pattern that was carved into it had changed colour. She lifted it to her face, peering closer. Small sections of the intertwining lines were now as red as Cerberus's eyes. She poked at one of them with her fingernail, pushing it in as far as she could.

A small hiss of steam puffed out of the key and she held her breath, wide-eyed. When nothing else happened she pulled her nail out of the metal, and turned the ball quickly, looking for another red bit. She found one, and repeated the action. Another puff of steam.

She kept going, turning the key, looking for the red sections of the pattern. Every time she found one more appeared, until she had lost count of how many little puffs of steam had been released. Then, finally, there was a loud click, and a tiny seam appeared, snaking its way all around the middle of the orb. Holding her breath, she pulled at each half of the line. The key fell open, the two halves joined by a tiny hinge, and in the centre was a vial full of thick, dark blue liquid. She picked it up gingerly, holding it to the orange light. Was it...?

She dropped the empty orb to the ground, trying to keep her hands from shaking as she carefully pulled the tiny stopper out and sniffed at the vial. Sulphur, she confirmed, her nose wrinkling. It was Hydra blood.

15

HERCULES

'Where is my cowardly daughter?' roared Hercules as he rolled under Eryx's swing, kicking out and catching him in the thigh. Eryx swore and darted out of reach as Hercules bounced back to his feet. Where was that red-haired bitch? The flash of white light he'd seen surely meant a god had taken her, but why?

Hercules glanced over his shoulder at Cerberus, prowling unhindered in front of the gates. He couldn't see Asterion. The minotaur was useless, he thought, sneering, and turned back to see whether the centaur had recovered herself yet. 'I will not kill either of you until she is here to see it!' he shouted as she pawed at the ground twenty feet away. If Lyssa wasn't here, he may as well end the Trials. He would have no trouble finding a way to kill her and crew publically once he was immortal.

He snapped his attention back towards the gates and Cerberus, thinking fast. The flames wouldn't bother Hercules himself, not with the lion skin protecting him. But he had no weapons, so he would have to take down the guard-dog with his bare hands. Excitement thrummed through him as his eyes settled on the neck of the central head. This would be child's play, he thought, and began to run towards the monster.

CERBERUS SAW HIM COMING, abandoned his pacing and dropped low on his haunches. A vicious snarl bubbled from all three mouths, their teeth dripping with dark red saliva as all six eyes focused on Hercules. Then another flash of white light forced his own eyes shut, and something hit him hard in the side. The air left his lungs as he flew towards the wing wall.

'This is it, Hercules!' Lyssa cried, as he landed hard, snapping his head around to see she that she had appeared out of nowhere, holding a glowing bow, fury and pain written on her face. 'This ends now,' she said, and for a moment he swore he could see purple crackling in her fierce eyes.

'At last!' he roared, and leaped to his feet. 'I'm going to enjoy this.'

GODS, she had become strong, he thought as they smashed into each other. He still had the advantage, though, his huge weight forcing her backwards as she locked her fists onto the lion skin as his shoulder-charge connected. Power rolled off her, and it wasn't Zeus's, he realised. It was different somehow, and a tiny flicker of doubt sparked in him as she pulled hard.

The lion skin shifted over him and he rolled his

shoulder hard, trying to dislodge her as he spun on the spot. Heat suddenly roared up around him and Lyssa let go abruptly as they stumbled into Cerberus's path. The guard-dog gave a single, terrifying bark and Hercules sprinted out of its way, back down the cavern. He registered Asterion, fighting with Eryx, as he passed, the quick half-giant ducking the minotaur's mace easily and landing blow after blow. The fool creature didn't deserve immortality, Hercules thought as he slowed down and turned back.

He barely had time to blink before Lyssa's fist smashed into his face.

16

HEDONE

Blood. Everywhere. Hedone felt like she was drowning in it. She couldn't control the fear, couldn't separate what was really happening from the images her mind was forcing on her. One minute she could see Hercules running through the cavern, the next he was a bloody twisted mess on the ground. Then he was back, wrestling with Lyssa, but her red hair was on fire and her arms were gone, replaced by blades dripping with gore...

'Stop!' Hedone sobbed, hiding her face in her hands. 'Please, please stop.' She took the biggest breaths she could manage. 'Come on, Hedone,' she pleaded with herself aloud. 'Come on. You came here for a reason. He might need you.' She clung to the thought of Hercules smiling and laughing, holding her tight, showering her face with kisses. Her hands began to shake less as she pressed them against her face. 'He might need you,' she repeated, willing the tears to stop rolling down her cheeks. She pictured the house she had decided they would live in, the gardens they would walk in, the pool they would swim in together.

Slowly, she lowered her hands from her face and searched for him. She couldn't look anywhere near the beast in front of the gates – just a glimpse of it was enough to overwhelm her and make her limbs stop working altogether – but she could see the centaur firing arrows in its direction, and Phyleus using a slingshot beside her. But the second she saw Hercules and Lyssa, she forgot anything else in the cavern existed.

They were moving fast, almost too fast to follow, punches and kicks flying at one another, each landed blow sending the other staggering. Hercules's face was twisted in an unnatural smile, as though he was enjoying the challenge. Lyssa's was a mask of hatred, and Hedone was sure she could see power in her eyes that had never been there before.

She forced herself to concentrate, to watch the fight, the suffocating fear of the cavern receding slightly as she focused on something else. But as she watched, a new, less irrational fear began to seep in. Lyssa was strong. And fast. When had that happened? There had been no question that Hercules was the strongest human in Olympus, so how was his daughter now able to match his every blow? Was it just the strength of her hatred for him? A flash of uncertainty shot through , Ladon's words ringing in her mind. Why did his daughter hate him so much? *Because he was an evil, cruel man, who had killed her family. He had hurt Evadne. He didn't help those in need. His temper was lethal.* She couldn't help the thoughts zipping through her head, facts that for a split second she knew beyond doubt were true. Horror rose inside her as Hercules's voice rang through the cavern.

'You will watch them all die, Lyssa, one by one!'

He is a killer. A murderer. A monster.

Then a wave of pain crashed through her head, so bad that nausea almost overcame her, and she gasped for breath. He needed her help. Hercules needed her help. He was a tool of the gods, misunderstood. The memory of his gentle hands on her face replaced the already-receding doubts, the memory of long conversations about their future overriding his words of war. Lyssa had somehow become stronger and now it was time to prove to her love that she could help him.

Steeling herself, Hedone grabbed the pack that she'd dropped from her back, and with shaking hands, untied the opening. Hercules had rolled his eyes with a small smile when he'd seen the bag, thinking it contained medical supplies. But she hadn't brought bandages and ambrosia like she'd told him. She'd brought Hippolyta's belt.

17

LYSSA

Lyssa jerked her head back out of Hercules's reach just in time to avoid his fist, ducking as she grabbed the front of his lion skin. She brought her own fist up, as hard as she could, relishing the crunch as it connected with the underside of his jaw, then pushing herself backwards, out of his reach. She expected him to come straight after her, but he stood his ground and let out a long, maniacal laugh.

'Little Lyssa has been training!' he said, his voice too high-pitched. His eyes were wild, and he spat blood onto the dark ground.

'No, Hercules. I'm just stronger than you now.' She knew the words were true as she said them. It was no longer just Rage pouring through her muscles, giving her strength. She had new speed, agility, a capacity to react to his movements earlier than she had been able to before. It was the ship's power, and it felt like the *Alastor*, ducking weaving and soaring through the skies. 'Are you scared, Hercules?' she shouted, dancing on her toes as they faced each other, energy coursing through her.

'Of you? Stupid little brat. I should have chased after you the night I killed your mother,' he snarled.

'You should have died the night you killed my mother, you fucking murderer!' she roared back, unable to control the flare of temper as she powered towards him. He kicked out as she reached him, his huge leg too big for her to dodge completely, and he caught her on the hip as she swerved. Pain blasted through her torso and she snarled as she rounded on him again. But he was too fast, and she felt his grip on her neck as she threw herself against his chest, trying to use her weight to knock him off balance. He stood firm, though, and she began to pummel his hand with both of hers as he lifted her off the ground slowly.

'Look at me, daughter,' he hissed, and she glared into his grey eyes, hatred swelling inside her as his fingers tightened around her neck. 'You know as well as I do, you're a killer. It's in your blood. You love the power.' She lifted her legs beneath her slowly, trying not to listen to his words. They may be true. There may be a killer deep inside her, just as her father's blood ran in her veins. But the only man she would ever kill would be him.

'I told you never to call me that!' she yelled, and swung her legs forward at the same time as punching out at his face with the flat of her hand. Her palm didn't reach his face, but her legs connected, hard enough for his grip to loosen. She grabbed his arm, solid muscle beneath her fingers, and pulled herself up, throwing her legs over his shoulder and feeling her stomach muscles wrench as she did so. A wave of fatigue swept through her and she snarled, forcing thoughts of her crew into her mind as she rolled herself up onto Hercules's back. A fresh surge of strength replaced the fatigue instantly, as he began to thrash, trying to shake her off. She got her arms around his neck, and began to squeeze, and he slowed in her grasp, throwing punches back at her that sailed harmlessly over her ducked head. She wrapped her knees around his broad back, clinging on. This had to end now.

'You wait, Lyssa,' he rasped, stumbling as he flailed his arms, his bulk making it impossible for him to reach her slight form. 'You'll enjoy squeezing the life from a body. You'll see.' His words almost made her loosen her grip in horror at the thought, but then she remembered who he was, and why she was doing this, and she squeezed harder. He clawed at her knees and she squirmed away, still keeping both arms tight around his neck.

'You won't hurt anyone else, Hercules. I don't care what it costs me, you won't hurt anyone else.'

The mighty Hercules dropped to his knees, the impact almost her knocking her off his back, but her feet scrabbled for purchase on the ground and she was able to tighten her hold even more. A wave of red crossed her vision as she felt him start to go limp in her arms, his fists no longer beating back at her. This really was it, she realised, bile rising in her throat. She was about to kill her own father.

SOMETHING SOLID HIT her side and before she knew what

happening, Lyssa was thrown from Hercules's back, soaring through the air towards the wall. She smashed into it, her spine making an awful crunching sound as she hit, then slid down to the ground. Black spots exploded into her vision, and she dimly heard Phyleus shouting. What had happened?

She forced herself to her knees, fighting nausea as pain swelled through her ribs. Looking up, she blinked, not sure of what she was seeing. Hedone was pulling Hercules to his feet, his face purple in the flickering orange light. And over her long black toga, she was wearing Hippolyta's great belt. She almost glowed with power, and for a brief moment Lyssa wanted to go and worship at her feet. She was utterly magnificent.

'Lyssa!'

She blinked again, and then Phyleus was next to her, one arm around her and the other trying to pull her to her feet. More pain lanced through her body and she cried out.

'You're hurt,' he said, panicked.

'I think it's just some broken ribs,' she gasped.

'Captain, he's going for Cerberus!' Eryx's bellow rang through the cavern, and Lyssa looked towards the gates. Hercules was sprinting towards the guard-dog.

18

ERYX

E ryx yelled as Asterion abandoned their fight, running after his captain. He was about to take off after them when Hedone's voice halted him in his tracks.

'You don't want to do that, Eryx. Why don't you just stand there and watch, like a good boy?' Her husky voice rippled over him, and a surge of desire overrode his battle-fuelled adrenaline. He *could* just watch. After all, he'd do anything to make Hedone happy, he thought, as she strode in front of him, smiling. Just look at her... She was perfect. 'Besides, Hercules has the lion skin. None of you could get close to that big flaming brute,' she purred. She was right, thought Eryx, relaxing. There was no need to do anything. They couldn't kill the dog anyway.

He watched as Asterion charged back and forth in front of the three heads, distracting them all, and Hercules crept around behind Cerberus. The guard-dog howled, and the sound cut through Eryx's haze of contentment. His eyes focused sharply.

'Evadne?' He turned to look for her, but Hedone coughed and he spun straight back to face her.

'Just watch,' she said. He obediently went back to watching Asterion, and frowned as one of the monster's dripping jaws caught his left leg. The minotaur wailed. Cerberus flicked his head, tossing Asterion high into the air, and Eryx watched as all three heads jerked up, snapping at the falling body. His face screwed up involuntarily as the furry flesh ripped, then each flaming jaw began shredding their own chunk of minotaur to bits on the ground in front of them.

A hail of arrows began raining down on Cerberus then, and Eryx swivelled his head around to see Nestor firing shot after shot at the dog. But he didn't even seem to notice them land as he chewed on his prey, and Eryx was sure the arrows were burning up before they even reached his bulging body. He couldn't just watch, he realised hazily. He was supposed to be doing something.

'Nestor, over here!' he shouted, and Hedone whirled back around to face him, frowning.

'Now, now, I thought I told you to watch quietly?'

Regret at upsetting her suddenly consumed him, and he dropped to his knees.

'I'm sorry, I'm so sorry,' he said, looking up at her as she sauntered closer to him.

'I should hope so. How will I reward you if you don't —' Her words were cut off and she gave a shriek of pain as an arrow thumped into her thigh.

Clarity crashed back down over Eryx. In an instant he sprang back to his feet and ran towards Lyssa.

'Why aren't you stopping him?' he shouted as he

reached her.

'I can't run,' wheezed Lyssa, her face pale.

'Where's the bow?' asked Phyleus urgently. 'The one Tenebrae gave you.'

Lyssa paused as she surveyed the cavern. Hercules had climbed up onto the dog's back, flames licking around the lion-skin cloak.

Panic, hatred and fear rose up in Eryx. 'We have to stop him!'

'It's over there,' Lyssa said, pointing.

'We need to get it,' Phyleus said, and pulled Lyssa, wincing, to her feet. 'We're almost out of time.'

'Captain!' Evadne shouted, running up to them, out of breath. 'You need to use this!' She held out an arrow, its end shining blue. Lyssa looked at her, confusion written on her face. 'Please, trust me, it's our last chance.'

'Captain, he's going to win,' roared Nestor, galloping towards them.

'Let me get on your back, Nestor,' Lyssa responded after a second's hesitation, and grabbed the arrow from Evadne's hand.

'Don't let any of the blue stuff touch you!' Evadne said desperately, as the centaur skidded to a stop and Phyleus helped Lyssa swing herself up.

'We're going to be too late, Captain,' said Nestor as they whirled back towards Cerberus. Hercules had both arms wrapped around the creature's thrashing central neck now, the other two heads snapping at him as he clung on.

'Shoot Hercules, not Cerberus!' Evadne yelled after them, as Nestor began to thunder across the cavern.

19

LYSSA

Lyssa gasped in pain as they galloped towards the glowing bow where it lay on the floor of the cavern. Nestor barely slowed when they reached it, flicking at it with her front hoof so that it flew up from the ground. Lyssa reached out, snatching it from the air, her ribs screaming in protest. She drew the bow back, resting the arrow carefully against her front hand as Nestor raced towards Hercules. She took aim, trying to keep herself as steady as she could, when she saw that the lights in the eyes of Cerberus's middle head were dimming.

'No,' she whispered. 'No, we can't be too late.' The eyes in the other two heads began dimming too, and dread took hold of Lyssa. Hercules was killing Cerberus. Hercules was going to win. *He was going to be immortal.* She saw him claw his way up the creature's neck as it began to collapse, raising himself so that his triumphant face could be seen over the dying flames. 'No!' she screamed, and loosed the arrow, straight at his face.

. . .

THE LIGHTS in Cerberus's eyes went out seconds before the arrow tore into Hercules's neck. The look of triumph on his face as he threw back the hood of his lion skin morphed suddenly, and pain was etched across his features for a moment, until he ripped the arrow out, throwing it to the ground with a clatter and raising his arms high in the air. Blood gushed from the wound, but time seemed to slow down as Lyssa watched it turn from deep scarlet to shining gold. *Ichor*. He'd done it. The trickle ebbed away to nothing, and Hercules let out a roaring bellow.

'You see me now, Father!' he shrieked. Nestor began to back up, and Lyssa closed her eyes, sure she was going to throw up. Hercules was immortal. He had won the Immortality Trials.

'We'll run, Lyssa. We'll run and we'll hide.' Phyleus's voice sounded in her mind and brutal pain, not physical but emotional, tore through her. The life she'd dared to want so badly, for her and her crew, was lost. And now they'd be lucky to survive for the next hour, let alone their natural lives. All the hope and strength she'd built up came crashing down and she couldn't breathe.

'I'm sorry,' she said, aloud, gasping for air. 'I'm sorry. I'm so, so sorry.' Tears rolled down her cheeks as Nestor turned towards the others, cantering past Hedone, who lay on the ground staring at the gold blood leaking from her thigh.

A scream ripped through the cavern, and Nestor leaped in shock, sending pain lancing through Lyssa's ribs again. Nestor spun to face the direction the sound had come from, and Lyssa clapped her hands over her ears to block it out. It was a terrible, primal noise and every fibre of her being wanted it to stop. Her skin was crawling.

And then she saw Hercules. He was bent over Cerberus's body, both his arms clamped over his head, and she realised the piercing wail was coming from him.

A flash of white light momentarily blinded her, and when it faded away she froze, unable to process what was happening. The fiery cavern and the winged demon gates were gone. They were at the Void, on the stage where they'd stood all those weeks ago. She was no longer on Nestor's back.

Lyssa looked around in panic and confusion. Emotions were spinning around her head so fast she felt sick, and it was only Phyleus's arm, wrapping instantly around her, that stopped her from sliding down onto the marble floor. Nestor was on her other side, and Len trotted to her fast. He handed her a small tonic from his bag. She drained it, and the black spots dancing in front of her eyes receded.

'Cap? You OK?'

'Broken ribs,' she muttered, looking at Abderos as he rolled up to her. 'What's happening?'

'I don't know.' She could hear the buzz of chatter and cheers and realised that the spectators who had come to see them at the starting ceremony were back. The area between the two stages was filled with citizens waving flags and shouting.

'Nobody knows,' growled Eryx, and she turned to see him standing beside Evadne, whose face was white under her straggly blue hair.

'I do,' she whispered. 'The blue stuff on the arrow was Hydra blood.'

'What... what does that mean?' Lyssa asked slowly.

'It means that although Hercules is our victor, he may not enjoy his immortality.' Athena's voice sang through her mind, and the others must have heard her too, because everyone's attention snapped to the other stage. The twelve gods materialised in front of their thrones, and the crowd fell instantly silent as they all bent low to their rulers.

'Congratulations, Hercules and Hedone, surviving crew members of the *Hybris* and winners of the Immortality Trials!' rang out the commentator's voice, and the crowd erupted into shouts and cheers. Lyssa felt weak as a gold platform rose to their right, moving out to hover over the crowd. But as she looked, she saw that Hercules wasn't standing victorious on the platform. He was hunched over, his face distorted in agony, his whole body shaking.

'Make it stop!' he shouted suddenly, and murmurs rippled through the crowd as the cheers died away.' Please,' Hercules gasped. 'Make it stop.'

Athena stood up from her throne, and her eyes fell on Lyssa's for a brief moment, before she looked at Hercules.

'Your ichor has been infected by Hydra blood, mighty Hercules,' the goddess said. 'The most poisonous substance known to Olympus. It would kill a mortal after a few short moments of the most crippling agony imaginable. But you... you are now immortal. And so you will not experience this pain for a few short moments, but for eternity.'

A cold shiver rippled through Lyssa as the words sank in. She turned to Evadne, who looked as sick as she felt.

'It was our only chance,' she whispered.

'He deserves it,' growled Eryx, and Nestor flicked her tail.

'He deserves every second,' the centaur agreed.

'Father, please, help me,' Hercules rasped from his golden platform.

'This competition has no rules and as such must play out naturally. To reverse what has happened would take the will of all twelve gods,' Zeus said, his booming voice sounding strained.

Poseidon barked a laugh.

'It would appear you have been *immortally wounded*, Hercules,' the god of the ocean said, not getting up from his chair. A lazy smile crossed his handsome face. 'An endless lifetime of agony. What a bore.'

'But...' Hedone stood up suddenly on the platform. She looked dazed, like she had even less idea of what had just happened than Lyssa did. 'But...' she stammered again, and Lyssa couldn't help feeling a surge of pity for her.

'Oh, my dear,' Aphrodite said, waving her hand and standing up. Her ruby lips stood out against her white face and her jet-black hair fell to her waist. 'It would be too cruel to saddle you with looking after this...' She gestured at Hercules's hunched form '... your whole life. I shall remove my influence. You are excused from your punishment.'

Aphrodite clicked her fingers, and Hedone turned slowly to Hercules, horror warping her beautiful face.

Her mouth moved silently as she stared at him. 'I hope you have learned your lesson, young lady. You do *not* come begging the goddess of love for favours. Or you may end up in love with the wrong person.'

Aphrodite looked at the crowd and beamed, then turned to Zeus. 'Now, Father, I believe we promised these citizens a feast? You'll all return in an hour.'

There was a familiar flash of white light, and then Lyssa was back on the *Alastor*.

20

LYSSA

'Lyssa... We're free. You did it,' Phyleus said. She stared at him, a strange numbness creeping over her as she sank down onto the planks of the deck.

'But he won,' she said. 'We lost. And now...'

'And now he will spend eternity in agony,' said Nestor, who was wearing the biggest smile Lyssa had ever seen on her severe face.

'I... I don't regret it,' said Evadne, kneeling in front of her. 'I didn't even know if it would work.'

'You're a genius, Evadne,' said Abderos, grinning at her. 'And, Cap, you're a great shot. You did it! You stopped Hercules!'

The words still wouldn't settle in her brain and she just stared at Abderos.

'Where's Epizon?' asked Eryx.

'He left,' she said, standing slowly. The pain in her ribs had lessened; the tonic Len gave her must be working. Why wasn't Epizon here? She needed him; he needed to be here for this.

'He's safe, though,' said Phyleus, and took her hand. 'It's over, Lyssa,' he said gently.

'It can't be. Epizon isn't here, and—' The flame dish on the quarterdeck flashed suddenly to life, and everybody looked up as an image materialised above the iron bowl.

'Nice work, Captain.' Epizon beamed. 'I knew you could do it.'

Lyssa looked from the flame dish to Phyleus. His face split into a grin.

'We're free. Hercules will never hurt anybody again.'

The numbness receded sharply, her daze lifting.

'We really did it!' she breathed, as a tidal wave of emotion crashed through her. She threw herself at Phyleus, and he yelled in surprise as she wrapped herself around him, squeezing him harder than she should. 'We did it!' she shouted again, releasing him, and turning to the fire dish. 'Ep, are you OK?' she called, running towards the quarterdeck, taking the stairs two at a time and ignoring the pain.

'Better than OK, Captain. And as soon as it's possible, I'll see you again. I reckon you're going to be impressed with this new realm. It looks like it's going to be something really special.' He was still beaming. 'I'm so proud of you, Lyssa,' he said.

Tears of happiness rolled down her face as she looked at him. 'And I'm happy for you, Ep.'

'Good. Now, go celebrate,' he said, and his image vanished from the dish.

'Captain, if I may,' said Nestor, and Lyssa turned back to the stairs. 'If Artemis will allow it, I would like to stay on your crew. As I mentioned, I live an endless life, and I have little to return to just now on Sagittarius.'

'Of course you can stay, Nestor,' Lyssa said, silent tears still running down her cheeks. 'We'd be honoured. You can have the position of gunner, when we spend some of the money from Zeus's golden apple and buy the ship a few treats.' She felt a ripple of energy pass through her body, and glanced up at the shimmering masts with a smile. *You've earned it*, she thought at the *Alastor*.

'You know, if you're looking to fill the first mate position...' said Phyleus, and he stepped forward, to the bottom of the little staircase.

'You know someone right for the job, huh?' she said, walking slowly down the first few steps and raising her eyebrows at him.

'I'd need to learn a little about ships,' he said, stepping onto the bottom plank and locking his eyes on hers. 'But I'm pretty close to someone who knows a lot about them. And I'm a fast learner.' He took another step up, as she took one down.

'The job's yours,' she whispered, as she grabbed the front of his shirt and kissed him.

21

EVADNE

The little blue longboat glided to a stop on the deck of the *Orion*. Evadne looked at Eryx as he sat, unmoving.

'It's OK, Eryx. He would have wanted this,' she said gently. He looked up at her, and the vulnerability on his scarred face made her heart melt. Some of the crippling guilt rolling through her seemed to lessen as she reached for his hand. 'We'll do it together.'

She stood up, tugging lightly at his hand. After a second's hesitation, he rose too, then slowly stepped over the side of the longboat, onto the deck. 'Try talking to the ship,' she said encouragingly, as she climbed out beside him.

'What if it doesn't want me?'

'Then we go back to the *Alastor*. Captain Lyssa would have us,' she said calmly.

But she didn't feel calm. She felt like her insides were made of jelly. She felt like her brain was as full as it could possibly be. She felt incredibly tired. And she feared she would never sleep again.

Eryx closed his eyes, and she let go of his hand, giving him space, though space was the last thing she wanted for herself. She didn't want time to think about what she had done to Hercules. To the man she had once respected. She dragged the painful memory of him in the galley with knife into her head, forcing herself to recall the justification for her actions. He was cruel and vicious and he deserved it, she told herself. But the image of him curled up, screaming in terrible agony, ripped through the memory. *Eternity*. He would experience that for eternity.

'You know, if the gods wanted to save him the suffering, they could,' said Eryx quietly, and she turned to him, surprised at this words. 'Athena pushed me and the Hydra key to you and Lyssa. They wanted this to happen.'

Hot tears began to burn the back of her eyes as she looked at him.

'Eternity,' she mumbled. 'An eternity of agony.'

'He's caused many others years of pain, Evadne. And would have caused many more. You saved lives.'

'You really think so?'

'I know so. I saw what he was capable of. He was broken.'

'What if I'm broken too?' she whispered, and she couldn't stop the tears falling as she voiced her deepest fear. 'What if I'm like him?'

Eryx's face creased up as he shook his head, closing the distance between them and pulling her into his enormous chest.

'What more could you do to prove that you're nothing like him? You've more than made up for your mistakes,' he said, as she sobbed into his shirt. 'You're... amazing.'

She snorted through her tears.

'I'm an idiot,' she said. Eryx's big hand snaked through her hair, turning her face up to his.

'You're brave and clever and I need you,' he said, and she saw tears glistening on his cheeks too.

'You do?'

'I do.'

'Eryx, I don't want to be the person you met at that feast. I don't want to be Evadne the gunner. I want... I want to start over. Can we start again?'

'Definitely. How about a game of dice?'

22

LYSSA

'So, what do we do now?' Phyleus asked Lyssa as she rubbed more delicious-smelling soap into her thick hair. She looked at him, leaning shirtless against the panelled wall of her washroom.

'Well, if you get into this bath with me, I could think of a few things...'

He grinned wickedly back at her, pulling the waist-band of his trousers tantalisingly low.

'While I'm definitely going to do that... I meant after your bath. You don't need to be a smuggler any more.'

Lyssa scowled at him.

'The money from the golden apple won't last forever. And smuggling is what we do on the *Alastor*. We fly across the whole of Olympus, bringing people things they need.'

'Well, maybe we could do something else. Something that still means we travel,' he said quickly. 'But less... illegal.'

Lyssa rolled her eyes.

'I knew getting involved with a prince was stupid,' she

muttered, and dunked her head under the water to wash out the soap. When she resurfaced, Phyleus was leaning on the edge of the tub, his face inches from hers. She squeaked in surprise and he laughed.

'I'm no good boy, Captain,' he whispered, his eyes darkening with lust. 'As you well know.' Her core clenched deliciously and she bit her lip. 'But Epizon had some great ideas about helping folk. We could really make a difference.'

She felt her heart beat faster as she looked into his deep brown eyes, so full of wit and fun, but also of kindness.

'Of course we can,' she said. 'And we will. No smuggling, until the drachmas run out,' she said solemnly. 'I promise.'

'Good,' he said, leaning over and kissing her gently.

'I love you, Lyssa,' he said in her mind.

She broke off the kiss, moving her wet hand to his stubbled jaw.

'I love you too. More than I ever believed was possible.'

'The skies of Olympus are ours,' he whispered.

THE END

THANK YOU

Thank you so much for reading, I hope you enjoyed it! If so, you would absolutely make my day if you could leave me a review on Amazon, they help me out so much! You can do that here.

If you want to find out what happened when Lyssa and her crew went to Leo to pick up Tenebrae then you can read the exclusive short story, Winds of Olympus, by signing up for my newsletter here. You'll also be the first to know about new releases!

READ ON for a secret bonus epilogue!

The Hades Trials will continue in the world of Olympus (featuring a few characters from The Immortality Trials) and is available for pre-order here!

ACKNOWLEDGMENTS

I decided to write this series after reading Marissa Meyer's incredible Lunar Chronicles. I'd always wanted to write a story about flying pirate ships, I'd always wanted to write Greek mythology retellings, and I wanted to write about more than one character. And after reading such an incredible series about a cyborg Cinderella from the moon I figured there was no reason at all not to give it a go.

And I'm so glad I did. None of this would have been possible without the unending support of my husband, who has become more involved in my writing than I could ever have hoped for. He is my rock, my lifeline, my everything. Thank you. I love you so much.

And I need to thank everybody who has helped and supported me. Brittany, Reena, you are both amazing. Your sharp eyes, honest feedback and positive support is invaluable to me. Anna, my amazing editor, Kyra, my fabulous proofreader, Elizabeth, my excellent narrator and Adina, my brilliant cover artist, thank you all so much for making writing a reality. And thank you to my friends who always ask how it's going when I talk to them.

But most of all, I want to thank YOU, lovely, lovely reader. Thank you so much for reading my work, you're making my dreams come true and allowing me to write more and more. I can't wait for you to read what's coming next.

Eliza xx

EPILOGUE

Hedone turned around, her stomach heaving again, but there was nothing left to bring up. Salty tears dripped onto her lips as she coughed, then sank back down into the scalding bathwater. It didn't help. Nothing would remove the memory of that monster. He had touched every part of her body, and no matter how raw she scrubbed her skin he lingered, his cold, cruel face huge before her.

She tried desperately to drag Theseus's image into her mind, but that brought fresh waves of pain that made her retch all over again. The memories battered her, images she had suppressed, ignored or refused to believe. Hercules breaking those centaurs' legs before they even left for the Trials, the terrified Evadne with her sawn-off hair, his brutal execution of the giants on his ship, the bodies littering the deck of the ship she adopted as her home. The words he had shrieked at his own daughter, his rage-filled eyes as he destroyed his chambers. Acidic bile rose in her throat again. Psyche's face floated before her, and painful longing overtook her, causing new tears to flood her eyes. What would she give for the woman's help now? But Psyche would never respect her again. Nobody would. And worst of all...

She heaved again, leaning her head over the side of the bath just in time. *She was immortal.* She had to spend her entire life living with this. With the knowledge that Aphrodite had manipulated and used her, forced her to abandon the people who loved her and give her body to a monster. The violation would stay with her for *eternity*. She tried to summon anger, tried to feel anything but utter despair, but she couldn't. Her mind was broken, useless.

'I can help you.' The voice startled her so much she began coughing again, hard. 'I can help you get revenge on the one who did this to you.'

'On Aphrodite? How?' she gasped, looking around the washroom frantically.

'I have my ways.'

'Who are you? Where are you?'

'That doesn't matter now. What matters is that you don't waste your immortality, and Aphrodite pays for her crimes.'